The Hunt For Hugo Dare

A HUGO DARE ADVENTURE

DAVID CODD

PROLOGUE

I was stuck up a tree.

No, that's not true. I wasn't stuck at all. I could climb down any time if I wanted to. Still, where would be the fun in that? There wouldn't be any. That was a fact.

I was perched about three branches up. Carefully, in case I lost my balance and fell, I leant forward and looked out over the gloomy grounds of the Pearly Gates Cemetery. I wasn't there as a mourner, but as an interested spectator.

An interested spectator to a funeral like no other.

Believe it or not, but the coffin which was about to be buried in the earth was completely empty. It was missing a body.

I knew this because the body was mine.

My name is Hugo Dare. Agent Minus Thirty-Five. Codename Pink Weasel. But you can call me Pinky.

I'm a spy. And that's exactly what I was doing now.

I was spying on my own funeral.

I waited until the coffin had been lowered into the open grave before I shifted my gaze to those in attendance. Aside from the stumbling, mumbling Father O'Garble (who, despite being on hand to oversee things, always seemed to be looking in the wrong direction), only three other people were there to grieve. One was my mother, one was my father and the other was the Big Cheese.

Two-thirds of those in attendance knew that I wasn't really dead, whilst the final third had planned the whole thing in the first place.

I watched as my mother, Doreen, removed a crusty, old tissue from somewhere up her sleeve and pressed it to her nose. The nasally blast that followed was both ridiculously loud and unnecessarily snotty. Never one to be outdone, my father, Dirk (also known as the greatest spy who never was), howled out loud like a wolf in the wild, before falling dramatically to his knees and burying his face in a molehill. Or maybe it was a huge pile of manure. It was impossible to tell from where I was perched.

Either way, one thing was clear. No one would miss me that much. Not even my own parents. So don't overdo it please.

Last but not least, I switched my attention to the Big Cheese. He was the Chief of SICK. The number one spymaster. And, perhaps most importantly of all, the man I called boss. Of the three, he was the only one who appeared both calm and composed as he stood by my graveside. He was also the only one who looked remarkably like a walrus, but that's a story for another time.

There was a wire fence that ran around the perimeter of the cemetery and, beyond that, an ugly crowd of undesirables lurking in the shadows. Like me, they had all turned up uninvited. Unlike me, however, they had no idea that I wasn't really in the coffin. They were only there for confirmation. Confirmation that I had died. And that was what was happening now. They could see it with their own eyes.

RIP Hugo Dare.

The service was coming to an end and there was no need for me to hang around a moment longer. Not unless I wanted to be spotted. And nobody wants to be spotted halfway up a tree on the day of their own funeral.

Scrambling down the trunk, I quickly checked that the coast was clear before I made an even quicker getaway. Maybe the Big Cheese's plan had worked. Maybe we really had convinced the rogues and wrong 'uns of Crooked Elbow that I was as dead as a dinosaur.

I had almost left the Pearly Gates Cemetery well and truly behind me when I heard a voice. It was coming from above. No, not up a tree. That was my trick.

'Wotcha', Stinky.'

I stopped suddenly. There was a girl sat on top of the wall beside the exit. She looked familiar. More than familiar, in fact. *Worryingly* familiar …

No way. Surely not. It couldn't be her. Not in a million years.

Oh. My mistake.

It could and it was.

Her name was Fatale De'Ath … and she was trouble!

1.'YOU'RE ELEVEN MINUTES LATE.'

Let's rewind things a little.

No, not too much. Just over a day. Twenty-seven hours and thirty-two minutes to be precise. Oh, and nineteen seconds. Don't forget about the nineteen seconds. I haven't. And neither should you. They could prove to be vitally important in the long run.

Allow me to set the scene. It was a dark and daunting Saturday morning in deepest, dampest winter and I, Hugo Dare, was stood in the middle of Crooked Green with a frown on my face and anything but a spring in my step. There was no one in sight and nothing to see. Just damp grass and bare trees and the occasional bird nest. Don't get me wrong; I wasn't there for the nature. I was there on business. The best kind of business.

Spy business.

The time was seven thirty-seven and I was supposed to be meeting someone at seven-thirty. Now, I'm no mathematician, but even I could figure out that she was late.

She being Brooke Keeper.

Brooke was the accountant for a large chunk of Crooked Elbow's criminal underworld. She looked after their finances, what money was going out and, more importantly, what money was coming in. That all changed, however, when she realised what she had got herself involved in. These were goons and gangsters she was dealing with. Hoods and heavies. They were rotten to the core and beastly to the bone. And Brooke … well, she wasn't. She was nice, not nasty. But she had got in way, way, way over her head and now she wanted out.

And that was where we came in.

We being SICK. Special Investigations into the Criminal Kind. We were the good guys. We agreed to help her, but we wanted something in return. That's the way it works, I'm afraid. You can either like it or lump it.

Of all the mad, bad and dangerous wrongdoers that used Brooke's services, there was one in particular that interested us the most.

His name was Deadly De'Ath and he had recently escaped from prison. No, not recently like earlier that day. That would be too recently for anyone's liking. I'm talking several weeks ago. Worse than that, I had been there to see him do it. He was halfway between the Crooked Clink and Sol's Solitary Slammer when, with the help of his number two, Layla Krool, he had somehow managed to slip through my fingers. Now we needed to find him and fast. Because if we didn't … well, let's not worry about that now. We'll save it for later on in the book. When we're really panicking.

If Brooke gave us everything she promised, all the facts and figures and dates and details, we would know more about De'Ath than we had ever known before. We might even discover where his current hideout was. And that, as far as the Big Cheese was concerned, was absolutely priceless in our efforts to get him back where he belonged.

Locked up. Behind Bars. From now until forever.

Seven thirty-eight.

I began to clap my hands and stamp my feet in time with the passing seconds, but not even that was enough to stop me from shivering. It was a bitterly breezy morning and, out there in the open, I was getting blasted left, right and centre by an unforgiving wind that found it far too easy to penetrate my school uniform. What's that? Yes, of course that's the same school uniform I had been wearing all week. Blazer, shirt, tie, shorts, the lot. I had even slept in it the previous evening. No, don't look at me like that. It's not because I'm lazy (well, maybe a little). It's just that getting dressed in the morning always seems to take far longer than it should do. Talking of which …

Seven thirty-nine.

I was starting to wonder if Brooke would ever arrive when I promptly decided she wouldn't. Not now. She had stood me up and left me in the lurch. Or maybe she had just got lost. Or fallen down a rabbit hole. Or been kidnapped by squirrels. Whatever the reason, she wasn't coming and I was freezing my fingertips off waiting for her to show. The way things were going it would probably take me the rest of the weekend to thaw out.

Seven-forty.

I was about to head for home and search for the hot water bottle when I spotted movement in the distance. At a guess, it was Brooke. It was the bunch of flowers that gave her away. They had been agreed beforehand so we could identify each other. I was carrying some, too, but, unlike hers which were freshly bought, mine were just weeds that I had picked from the side of the road and then stuffed into my back pocket.

Seven forty-one.

'You're eleven minutes late,' I called out.

Dressed in a huge, padded jacket that made her look at least three times the size she really was, and a baseball cap pulled so low over her face that I doubted she could see anything above her chin, Brooke almost fell over her own feet at the sound of my voice. It was only when she recovered that I noticed it wasn't just the flowers she had brought with her. There was something else. Something big, brown and bulky.

'Going anywhere nice?' I asked, nodding towards the suitcase she was dragging behind her.

'No … not nice … not nice whatsoever.' Twitchier than a bird spotter on the first day of spring, Brooke stopped without warning and glanced over both shoulders. 'Are you Pink Weasel?' she asked nervously.

'I am indeed,' I said. 'I'm not one to bend my own boomerang, but I'm SICK's most talented teenage spy. You're in good hands, even if they are a little dirty. And surprisingly sticky. Don't panic; I'll wash them later. And you don't have to fret about anybody seeing us here either. We're perfectly safe. So, what have you got for me? Nothing too heavy, I hope. A file or folder? A memory stick perhaps? Or maybe—'

'This!' Brooke lifted the suitcase up off the ground. 'This is for you.'

'For me?' I screwed up my face. 'Call me ungrateful, but I wasn't expecting something quite so … luggage-like!'

'It's not the suitcase that's important,' explained Brooke. 'It's what's inside it. A laptop. I had to hide it in case anybody saw me. In hindsight, I could probably have used a shopping bag. Oh, this is all too much for me to deal with. I really shouldn't be here … not with you … a spy of all people.'

'You worry too much,' I said, trying to reassure her. 'Just pass me the suitcase and you can get on with the rest of your life. It's that simple. With any luck, you won't have to work for any of those rotters ever again … and that's because they'll all be serving time in the Crooked Clink! Every last one of them. Even Deadly De'Ath.'

'Don't say that!' bleated Brooke. 'You only have to whisper his name and he knows where to find you!'

'That's clever,' I said, raising an eyebrow. 'And completely impossible, of course. Still, don't let any of that put you off giving me that suitcase … now … please.'

Brooke snatched a breath. 'Yes, you're right. You can have it. I trust you.'

'Really?' I gasped. Wow. That was a turn up. Strange as it seemed, things appeared to be going to plan. I say that because, whatever I did, however I did it, there was always a hiccup or three to contend with somewhere along the line. An unexpected problem that urgently needed solving. Some kind of minor complication blocking my way.

Not this time, though. This time it was all plain sailing. Wait …

I had already stepped forward with my hand out-stretched, ready to take the suitcase, when Brooke's mouth fell open. I could only imagine that she had spotted something over my shoulder. Something so shocking, so frightening that her face turned white and she began to shake. Either that or she had seen me up close for the very first time. It's nothing to be proud of, but I do tend to have that effect on people.

'What's wrong? I asked.

Brooke ignored the question and chose, instead, to throw the suitcase straight at my face.

I lifted my hands and swatted it away before it hit me on the nose. By the time I had switched my attention back to Brooke, she was already on the move.

'Where are you going?' I called out.

Brooke had almost vanished from view when I heard something coming up behind me.

I spun around. Two men had appeared from nowhere. Big men. With big arms. Big legs. Big ears. Big everything except their brains. That was just a guess, but I'd be surprised if I was wrong. Both were dressed identically in dark suits, white shirts and black shiny shoes. Oh, and sunglasses. Why? There wasn't even a squeak of any sunshine today. Or tomorrow. Or the week after that. Believe it or not, but I didn't even know they sold sunglasses in Crooked Elbow (umbrellas, however, are incredibly popular).

I hesitated for a moment, unsure if the two men mountains were just out for an early morning stroll, before I realised they were both carrying weapons.

This was that hiccup I was telling you about. The unexpected problem. The minor complication.

No, two big men makes two complications.

Two *major* complications.

2.'THERE'S NO NEED TO SAY THANK YOU.'

Most ordinary people would've turned around and scarpered.

But then I'm not like most ordinary people. No, I'm different. Unique. One of a kind. In a good way, of course. Not peculiar in the slightest. And that was why I stayed exactly where I was and studied the two men a little more closely. I figured I had time. Truth is, they weren't really moving that fast. Like a pair of muscle-bound, fully-clothed ducks, they were waddling rather than running towards me.

I'll start with the man on the left. Let's call him faceless goon number one, shall we? No, you're right. That's way too much of a mouthful. How about something easier to swallow? Something like … Wally? Yes, that'll do nicely.

Wally was carrying a handgun. Not a good start. He was also clutching hold of an inhaler which, all things considered, was probably to my advantage. Either he had mistaken it for another gun and picked it up by accident (unlikely) or he needed it to help him breathe. I decided it was the latter of the two when he stuck it in his mouth and gave it a good blast. A moment later he was back wheezing again, which – nothing personal, Wally – pleased me immensely.

Stan's weapon, meanwhile, was a small, wooden baton, similar to a policeman's truncheon. What's that? Oh, you're wondering who Stan is? Faceless goon number two, of course. He had the same thick neck, huge arms and bruised knuckles as Wheezing Wally … and a handkerchief. Stan sneezed into it once and slightly stumbled. Then he sneezed again and almost fell over. If he sneezed for a third time, I was sure he'd end up sunglasses first in the grass. As satisfying as it would have been for me to wait around until that happened, I just couldn't take the risk. Both goons were armed and I wasn't. And that's why I grabbed the suitcase out of the muddy puddle it had landed in and set off after Brooke Keeper as fast as my school shoes would take me.

Maybe she knew a secret way out of Crooked Green. Some kind of hidden escape route that I could follow her through, leaving Stan and Wally none the wiser as to our whereabouts.

Funnily enough, she didn't.

It took me no time at all to catch up with her … and even less time than that to realise that all Brooke was doing was running around in circles.

'Friends of yours?' I asked, gesturing behind me at the two goons. Weapons raised, Stan and Wally were hot on our heels. Well, they were more warm than hot. Slightly tepid even. Okay, so if I'm being honest they had barely shifted out of duck waddling mode, but I'm trying to add some tension.

'Not friends,' panted Brooke, as she began her second lap of Crooked Green. 'But I do know who they work for.'

I waited for her to spill the beans. And then waited some more. And a little bit more after that. I was still waiting, in fact, when I decided that waiting wasn't really my *thing*. 'Is it a secret?' I blurted out. 'Because if it isn't I'd very much like to know. Sooner rather than later if possible. Today preferably. This minute would be nice.'

'Victor Smog,' revealed Brooke, struggling to speak. 'They work for Victor Smog.'

'Victor Smog?' I screwed up my face. The name rang a bell; it just wasn't chiming loud enough for me to hear.

Brooke began to slow so she could catch her breath. 'You look confused,' she said. 'Everybody knows Victor Smog. I was his accountant long before he became the most powerful businessman in Crooked Elbow. Oh, come on. You must have heard of Smog Skyscrapers? Smog Space Shuttles? Smog Speedboats? Smog Sausages?'

Ding-a-ling-a-ling. That bell just got a whole lot louder.

'Smog Sausages?' I cried. 'I love Smog Sausages. They're my favourites. Do you think Stan and Wally might have a pack or six hidden inside their trousers?'

Now it was Brooke's turn to look confused. 'Stan and who?'

'It doesn't matter.' I lifted my elbow and peered under my armpit. Sneezing and wheezing with every step, the two faceless goons were closer than I would've liked. 'What do you think they want?' I wondered.

'The suitcase, of course!' remarked Brooke. 'Just give it to them.'

'No way,' I replied, gripping hold of the handle as I ran. 'There's absolutely zero chance whatsoever that I'm going to give this to those two … whoa!'

The momentary *crack* of a gunshot stopped me mid-sentence. My legs, though, kept on moving, swerving violently from side to side for fear of being hit. I had no idea where the bullet ended up, but it didn't end up in me. Or Brooke, for that matter. She did, however, decide that swerving wasn't really for her and dived head first into the nearest bush. It was both thick and thorny in equal measures. Painful to say the least. Something that Brooke would undoubtedly agree with judging by the squeals and shrieks that followed.

'There's no need to shoot,' I yelled over my shoulder. 'You can have the suitcase. It's not that nice anyway … quite tatty really … yikes!'

I ducked down as another ear-splitting *crack* echoed around Crooked Green. This was more serious than I had first figured. Seriously serious.

Wary of a third shot being more accurate than the first two, I tried to speed things up a little. It didn't work. I had barely broken into a sprint when I completely lost my footing and slipped over in the wet grass. Rolling onto my back, I was horrified to find that Sneezing Stan and Wheezing Wally were now almost upon me. My first reaction was to slide the suitcase towards them (even if the suitcase's reaction was to come up short in the mud).

'Have it,' I said. 'It's all yours. There's no need to say thank you.'

They didn't.

Wally took a puff on his inhaler before he lifted the gun, whilst Stan sneezed one more time before he slapped the baton against the palm of his hand.

I was wrong. This wasn't seriously serious at all. No, it was worse than that. Much worse.

Life threateningly worse.

3.'WHAT ARE YOU WAITING FOR?'

I can talk my way out of any situation.

It's one of my many skills. Well, one of my *only* skills if I'm being honest. Okay, so it's not even a skill, is it? Not really. Still, I'm going to do it anyway so you may as well sit back and take notes because this is going to be something special indeed.

I took the deepest breath imaginable and then ...

'Do you make them? The sausages, I mean. Because that would be my dream job. That and professional crocodile wrestler. Not alligators, though. They're a whole different species altogether. Admittedly, crocodiles can be the more bad-tempered of the two, but I do prefer their lovely toothy grin, not to mention their snout, which, as snouts go, is far nicer. Ah, this is enjoyable, isn't it? You and you and me ... just the three of us ... chatting like old chums ... shooting the breeze like good buddies. Listen, goons, if either of you want to put down your weapons, turn around and close your eyes, then just go ahead and do it. I won't think bad of you. I promise.'

I stopped talking so they could do as I asked ... and then started again when they didn't!

'Okay, so you're not that friendly then,' I muttered. 'And you don't speak either. Brilliant. You're not making things easy for me, are you?'

Wally answered that particular question by pointing the gun straight at my face.

'Whoa! Now you're *really* making things not easy for me,' I whimpered. 'There's no need for any of this. The suitcase is by your feet … what are you waiting for?'

Wally turned towards his partner and shrugged. I couldn't be certain, but it seemed as if they had no interest in the suitcase whatsoever.

But they did have an interest in me.

I jumped to my feet, ready to fight. Then I sat back down again because it was far too slippery and, besides, I had nothing to fight with. Only my bare hands. And they were no match for a handgun and a baton (they were barely a match for a water pistol and a celery stick).

Both sullenly silent *and* uncomfortably violent, Wheezing Wally and Sneezing Stan made for one heck of an imposing double act. I knew I had to do something before it was too late. Something swift. Something smart. Something that would put a stop to this once and for all.

With nothing to lose, I snatched blindly at the nearest thing to hand and threw it as hard as I could at the advancing goons. I regretted it instantly when I realised it was nothing more than a thick clump of grass. I was about to grab something else when the clump hit Stan full in the face. Without warning, his nostrils twitched and his bottom lip began to tremble.

Then he sneezed.

Now I'm no expert when it comes to mouth explosions, but this one seemed particularly powerful. Powerful enough to make Stan drop both his handkerchief and his baton as he swung his arms in a wide arc, trying desperately to steady himself. The handkerchief floated gently to the ground, whilst the baton struck Wally firmly across the back of the head. It was an accident, of course, but Wally didn't know that.

But then he didn't know anything. Not anymore. Not now he had been knocked unconscious.

Stan was still sneezing uncontrollably as Wally took a tumble and ended up beside me in the mud. With his eyes closed, Stan then staggered forward and tripped over his fallen friend. Now he really did hit the ground sunglasses-first. I knew it would happen eventually.

Nobody moved. Not even an inch. I shuffled over to the two faceless goons and gave them a quick once over. Both were out cold, and it was all because of a simple clump of grass. Even by my standards, that was highly impressive. I don't know how I do it sometimes. I guess I'm just an exceptionally talented super spy (or just really, really lucky. I'll let you decide.)

Four seconds later I was up and away with the suitcase by my side. I had to move fast before Wally or Stan started to stir. Unlike Brooke, however, I had figured out how to leave Crooked Green without running around in circles. Not only that, but I knew exactly where I was heading next.

The SICK Bucket.

I'll see you there.

4.'LESS WRITING,
MORE FIGHTING.'

Where have you been?

You only had to turn the page. Nothing too difficult. It's rude to leave me waiting that long, especially after the journey I've just had. Don't ask me why, but it seemed as if I was being watched at every turn. Oh, my mistake. I know exactly why it felt like that. Because I *was* being watched. And not just by rogues and wrong 'uns either. I'm talking window cleaners … traffic wardens … ambulance drivers … dog walkers. Even the dogs themselves. For some reason that I couldn't quite put my finger on, anybody and everybody I passed seemed to take more than a fleeting interest in yours truly. I checked my face in a shop window just to be sure, but there was nothing unusual dangling from my nose or dribbling out the corner of my mouth. As far as I could tell I looked perfectly normal (or as perfectly normal as I ever looked at least).

First Sneezing Stan and Wheezing Wally and now this. It didn't make sense. And that's probably why I was a little snappy when you finally decided to show up.

Still, you're here now so I might as well get on with it.

I was stood outside The Impossible Pizza takeaway. No, don't look at me like that. I'm not thinking about my belly and that's the end of it. Well, I wasn't. I am now, of course, but that's your fault for reminding me.

Let's get one thing straight. The Impossible Pizza is like no other takeaway on the planet. Firstly, it's never been open for business. Not once. Not ever. And secondly – and most important of all – it leads all the way to the SICK Bucket. That's SICK's secret underground headquarters to those in the know. And to those who aren't, it's SICK's secret underground headquarters. There. We're all in the know now.

More than a little on edge after my curious journey, I wandered nervously up to the entrance and twisted the knob three times to my left and then twice to my right. There was a *click* as the door slowly opened. I was just as nervous as I slipped inside.

Then I was something else entirely.

I was petrified.

I had barely closed the door behind me when I found myself face-to-face with SICK's first line of defence.

Impossible Rita.

With her close-cropped hair, wild eyes and even wilder temper, Rita was the head chef of a takeaway that had never been open (yeah, try and figure that one out). Angry both inside and out, she liked to attack first and ask questions later. And that was exactly what she was about to do when I held up the suitcase.

'Stop!' I said firmly. 'I've got this.'

Shuddering to a halt, Rita grabbed the suitcase from out of my hands and then whacked me over the head with it.

'Ouch!' I cried. 'Why would you do that?'

'Why wouldn't I?' Rita shrugged. 'Now, what's the password?'

'Forget about the password,' I said grumpily. 'Just put the suitcase down before you damage what's inside.'

'You shouldn't have given it to me if you didn't want me to use it,' shot back Rita. Turning sharply, she stormed across the takeaway in a furious rage. 'Happy now?' she said, placing the suitcase down on the counter.

'Not really,' I muttered.

'Good.' With that, Impossible Rita spun me around by my shoulders, tripped me over and then sat on my back. It all happened so fast there was nothing I could do about it.

'Get off,' I grumbled.

'Not yet,' said Rita, refusing to shift. 'Not until you tell me the new password.'

New password. 'Let me see,' I muttered. 'I think I know it … I'm sure I do, in fact … is it … *I'm SICK of it?*'

'I don't know,' replied Rita. 'Are you SICK of it?'

'Of course I'm not,' I moaned through gritted teeth.

'Then why say it?' yelled Rita.

'Because it's the password,' I hollered back at her. 'I'm SICK of it. I … am … SICK … of … it! And I'm sick of you!'

'Okay, you don't have to go on about it.' At the same time, Rita climbed off my back and dragged me to my feet. 'You can go now,' she said. 'You make my takeaway look untidy.'

I pulled a face at her as I recovered the suitcase from the counter and hurried towards the rubbish chute.

Yes, the rubbish chute.

As well as being revoltingly smelly, it was also the only way to access the SICK Bucket.

Careful not to fall, I climbed in feet first and tried to steady myself against the slimy sides of the chute. Then I let go by accident. All of a sudden I was hurtling downwards at a speed so terrifying that my eyeballs felt as if they were coming out of my ears. It was horrible, yes, but I knew it wouldn't last for long before … wait for it … any moment now … I landed on something soft and spongy and unmistakeably human.

Roland 'Rumble' Robinson was SICK's second line of defence.

As wide as he was tall, former wrestler Rumble stalked the exit to the rubbish chute whilst acting as a trampoline for all new arrivals. Three bounces later he put me back on my feet so he could give me an all over body search. He moved quickly and quietly. It tickled a little, but I chose not to complain (although that was largely because I didn't dare to).

Body search over, I bid Rumble a fond farewell and set off across the length of the SICK Bucket towards the Big Cheese's Pantry (that's his office; not where he stores his packed lunch.) I shivered as I drew level with the desk that was normally reserved for his secretary. I say normally because today it was empty.

And long may it stay that way.

I know it's hard to believe, but I had never seen eye-to-eye with any of the Big Cheese's previous secretaries. One had tried to kill me, whilst the other had tried to kill me as well. Thankfully, I had a one hundred-per-cent survival record. Two out of two had failed. But that was nothing to be proud of.

I had almost left the desk behind me when I heard a curious scraping sound coming from somewhere underneath it. I stopped walking and listened carefully. If anything, it sounded like a mouse. And even if the mouse in question liked the Big Cheese, the Big Cheese certainly wouldn't like the mouse. If only I could find a way to lure the furry fellow into my hands, then I could put it somewhere it couldn't escape. Like in the pocket of my blazer. Or even down my shorts. Yes, that would do the trick. I can't imagine what could possibly go wrong down there.

Walking on tiptoes, I moved cautiously at first so as not to scare the creature away. The scraping seemed to increase with every step … until … I could finally see it.

It was bigger than a mouse. Much bigger, in fact. Almost as big as a …

I screamed in horror as a human head popped up from under the desk. As if that wasn't bad enough, I screamed again when a body followed the head and the body belonged to a woman. Short in stature and round in shape, she had bobbed black hair, big eyes hidden behind a pair of thick spectacles, and an unnaturally wide mouth like a famished frog about to feast.

'Sorry,' she said, smiling awkwardly as she clambered to her feet. 'I didn't mean to frighten you.'

'You didn't,' I replied hastily. 'I'm ... um ... positively unfrightenable.'

'Oh, really,' said the woman, puzzled. 'I thought I heard you scream.'

'Scream? Me? No ... well, maybe ... maybe I did,' I had to admit. 'But that's because I ... erm ... always scream. It's a hobby of mine. I do it all week long. Monday to Sunday without fail. But never when I'm frightened.'

'Have you finished?' laughed the woman.

'Almost,' I said. 'Just one last thing. Why were you hiding under that desk?'

'I wasn't hiding – I was fixing it.' The woman held out her hand and showed me a screwdriver. 'The legs were a little loose so I decided to tighten them,' she explained. 'Rather that than have it collapse on me. It is my desk, after all.'

'Your desk?' I screwed up my face. 'No, this desk belongs to the Big Cheese's secretary.'

'That's right,' nodded the woman. 'I'm Poppy. Poppy Wildheart. The Big Cheese's new secretary. Well, I'm actually his personal assistant, but it's much the same thing ... oh, you're leaving. Was it something I said?'

'What makes you think that?' Using the suitcase as a barrier between us, I had started to shuffle sideways towards the Pantry. 'Well, maybe it was,' I mumbled. 'Just a bit ... a tiny bit ... a teeny, tiny, terrifying bit. The thing is, I haven't always been on the best of terms with the Big Cheese's previous secretaries. They didn't like me. No, that's only half the story. The other half is they wanted me dead. And they nearly got their wish.'

'I'm not like them,' Poppy insisted. 'Besides, if I wanted you dead I would've done it by now.'

I tried to speak, but the words got stuck in my throat.

'That came out wrong,' said Poppy hastily. 'I'm actually here to help – not hurt. Although, I am a little more hands on than the others. Less writing, more fighting. Now, Hugo, if you'd be so kind …'

I flinched as Poppy squeezed past me and opened the door to the Pantry.

'You know my name?' I said warily.

'Of course,' Poppy grinned. 'It's my job to know your name. It's also my job to keep things moving. And that's why you can go in now. The Big Cheese is ready for you.'

I did as she asked and wandered in. Not before I'd taken one last look at Poppy Wildheart, however. As first impressions go, the Big Cheese had chosen well. She seemed like the perfect personal assistant.

And that was probably why I didn't trust her in the slightest.

5.'GOOD FOR THE MIND, BODY AND SOUL.'

The first thing I saw when I entered the Pantry was the Big Cheese.

He was stood on his writing table. Wobbling gently from side to side, he had his hands on his hips and one foot flat against the side of his opposite knee. Not only that, but his eyes were closed, his bald head was rubbing against the ceiling and he was sweating so much it was dripping from the tips of his droopy moustache onto the carpet.

I coughed once to get his attention, but he completely ignored me. Bit rude. And that was why I coughed four more times before one of his eyes finally opened.

'Oh, what is it, young Dare?' he moaned. 'Can't you see I'm busy?'

'I can see you're something, sir, but it's not busy,' I replied. 'Are you feeling okay?'

'Why wouldn't I be?' the Big Cheese shot back. 'They call this the tree.'

'I call it a disaster waiting to happen,' I remarked accurately.

'You would do.' Scrambling down from the table, the Big Cheese barely paused for breath before he knelt down and placed his chin on the carpet. 'Have you never seen a grown man do yoga before?' he bellowed. 'I'm trying it for the first time. This one's called the caterpillar. It's harder than it looks.'

'Let's just hope it's not as painful as it looks,' I muttered. Right on cue, I heard an uncomfortably loud *snap*.

'That's supposed to happen,' grimaced the Big Cheese, rubbing his spine. 'Yoga's good for the mind, body and soul.'

'But not so good for your trousers, sir,' I added. 'I think they might have split.'

The Big Cheese stopped stretching and lifted his head. 'Enough of the wisecracks, young Dare. Why are you here and how long do you think it'll be before you leave?'

I dragged the suitcase across the carpet and plonked it down by his forehead. 'I'm here because of this.'

'I didn't know you were going on holiday,' the Big Cheese boomed. 'Still, I'm sure we won't miss you too much. If at all. And there's no need to send a postcard. I'll be far too busy to read it anyway. Busy doing my yoga.'

'Slow down, sir,' I said. 'I'm not going anywhere. Truth is, this isn't my suitcase.'

With that, I hopped over the Big Cheese and placed the object in question on the table. There was a zip running all the way around the outside. It was stiff, but not so stiff that I couldn't get it moving just four yanks, three tugs and two pulls later.

Panting for breath, the Big Cheese finally stood up and

straightened his cravat. 'What in the wild world of weirdness is that?' he asked, peering inside the suitcase.

'It's a laptop, sir,' I replied.

The Big Cheese looked anything but impressed. 'What's a laptop?'

'A computer, sir,' I explained. 'Everybody's got one.'

'Everybody … except me,' the Big Cheese shrugged. 'And I don't want one either. I suppose it's the thought that counts, young Dare, but I'd rather you just took it back to where it came from—'

'It's not a present, sir,' I said quickly. 'Brooke Keeper gave it to me shortly before she jumped into a bush. As far as I'm aware everything we need to know about Deadly De'Ath is stored somewhere on it.'

The Big Cheese stopped to stroke his moustache. 'I won't lie,' he said eventually. 'I was expecting you to return with something a little … smaller. And thinner. And more paper-like. Like a piece of paper for example. A piece of paper with words and numbers on it. This, however … this computer of the lap thingamajig … leaves me as cold as icicles on a reindeer. Technology and I do not go hand in hand, young Dare. If anything, we turn our backs on one another and walk away. We agree never to meet again. If we do, though, purely by chance, we simply cross the road and avoid eye contact. Now, I'm not saying we don't share the odd phone call at Christmas … a birthday card perhaps … but that's all. We mean nothing to each other. Sad times indeed.'

I tried not to stare as a single tear trickled down the Big Cheese's cheek.

'It's just a laptop, sir,' I said eventually. 'It's not worth getting emotional about. Surely there's somebody else in the SICK Bucket ... I don't know, a computer expert for instance ... who can extract the information from it.'

'Not that I know of,' replied the Big Cheese stubbornly.

'What? Nobody?' I screwed up my face. 'There must be.'

'No, there mustn't ... because there isn't,' argued the Big Cheese. 'We're spies, young Dare. We sneak about in the shadows and blend into the background. We watch and wait. We look, listen and learn. We talk in code and leave messages that are impossible to decipher. We are not ... I repeat, we are not ... computer people.'

'What about your new personal assistant?' I asked, gesturing over my shoulder. 'I'm guessing you found out if she could use a computer before you employed her.'

'Maybe I did, maybe I didn't.' The Big Cheese hesitated. 'Okay, so I didn't ... and I'm not going to ask her now. Don't be fooled by her friendly face and dove-like demeanour, young Dare. Poppy Wildheart prefers to punch people rather than keys on a keyboard. Yes, I was shocked, too. I was even more shocked when she attacked Rumble the first time they met. Don't ask me why, but she wasn't particularly pleased to land on a human trampoline at the bottom of the rubbish chute. And that's why she karate-chopped him in the neck.'

'Poor Rumble,' I said.

'He'll get over it,' shrugged the Big Cheese. 'I know I have. Right ... let me think ... there is somebody we could use. An outside source. He's an expert when it comes to all things technological. I'm sure he'll take a look at this lap of the top contraption for the right price. He'll probably even turn it on for us if we ask politely.'

'What's his name?' I wondered.

'Chip,' replied the Big Cheese. 'Computer Chip. He lives at the top of a huge apartment block on the pleasant side of Crooked Elbow. He works quite late into the night, though, so you might want to leave it an hour or two …'

'Leave *what* an hour or two, sir?' I asked.

'Leave it an hour or two before you go and drop off the taplop … loptap … toplap … laptop,' insisted the Big Cheese, fourth time lucky. 'And you can drop off that hideous suitcase as well. Chip can have that for free. Really, young Dare, there's no need to pull such an unnaturally freakish face at me. You didn't really think I'd be going to see Chip myself, did you?'

Well, yes. Obviously. Not that I said that, though. 'You'll have to give me the full address, sir,' I sighed instead.

'Number one-hundred and ninety-three Smog Suites,' revealed the Big Cheese. 'Their apartment is on the top floor. The thirty-seventh. It's so high up it's practically in the clouds.'

'Smog Suites?' I put two and two together, doubled it and removed seven until I was finally left with one.

And that one was Victor Smog.

'There was somebody else at Crooked Green when I met Brooke,' I began. 'No, make that *two* somebody elses. Two faceless goons. They worked for Victor Smog.'

'And?' cried the Big Cheese. 'You are aware that Smog is

one of the most powerful businessmen in Crooked Elbow, aren't you? It makes sense that he would send a couple of his minions to follow Brooke if he found out what she was up to. Still, at least they didn't get their hands on the suitcase.'

'Only because they didn't want it,' I argued. 'The only thing they were interested in was me. Do you think it's anything to be concerned about, sir?'

'Do I look concerned?' laughed the Big Cheese.

'Okay, is it anything for *me* to be concerned about?' I asked instead.

The Big Cheese waved the question away with a waft of his fat fingers. 'No, nay and never,' he barked. 'Think about it, young Dare. You're like a new-born baby on the spy scene. You know less than nothing. Nothing that anybody else wants to know anyway. At a guess, those two goons just took a dislike to your face. I often feel that way myself when I look at you. Now, run along and leave me be so I can get back to the matter at hand. I've got a cat, a cow and camel to squeeze in before the morning's out.'

I screwed up my face. 'That's quite some appetite, sir.'

'It's yoga,' growled the Big Cheese.

'Good for the mind, body and soul,' I muttered to myself. And it was my own mind, body and soul that were worrying me the most as I turned to leave the Pantry. The Big Cheese may have found it easy to dismiss, but Victor Smog had almost certainly sent Wheezing Wally and Sneezing Stan to pick me up. And not in a cuddly kind of way either.

I had no idea why, but I, Hugo Dare, was a wanted man.

No, a wanted boy.

No, a wanted spy. Yes, that's better.

Shall we leave it there and move on?

6. 'WHAT'S THE WORST THAT CAN HAPPEN?'

The Big Cheese had suggested I leave it an hour or two before I go and see Computer Chip.

That was a good idea, largely because there was somewhere else I wanted to go first. Don't worry; I'm not heading far. Only a few steps in the right direction.

The Bulging Bellyful café hadn't always been opposite The Impossible Pizza, but right now, at this very moment in time, it most certainly was. Some people would even say that it was all thanks to me, not that I'd ever choose to admit it. The café had a reputation, you see. A reputation for horrendously horrible food that, when eaten, could easily lead to either a day stuck on the lavatory, a week in hospital, or worst case scenario, a lifetime in a coffin. The poisonings had been so bad that the owners, Grot and Grunt, had been banished to the depths of Elbow's End for crimes against cooking. That was where I had last met them. Grot had helped me to escape (even if she didn't know a thing about it) so I offered to put in a good word on my return. I told the Big Cheese, the Big Cheese told the Mayor, and the Mayor told them to come home.

And that was why the Bulging Bellyful was now back where it belonged … and it was all my fault!

I dragged the suitcase across the road and peered through the café's grimy glass window. It was empty inside, but that was hardly a surprise. It's not easy to attract customers if poisoning people is what you're best known for. Thankfully, I wasn't there to eat. No, not even I'm that greedy.

Pressing down on the handle, I stepped inside and tried not to breathe in the rancid air that hovered around me.

'I reckoned it were ya, Pinky.'

I looked up and spotted Grot lurking behind the counter. She was the face of the business … and what a frightful face it was! You can skip this bit if you like because it's not particularly pleasant. Right, deep breath …

From top to bottom (don't mention her bottom), Grot had purple hair that hung limply over eyes that pointed in different directions, a hooked nose that was covered in warts, skin the colour of week-old cat sick, crumpled cauliflower ears, too many chins to count and a neck that was completely swallowed up by her hunched shoulders. I know that's a lot to take in, but I'm trying to write fast so I don't put you off. The last thing I want is you disappearing to the bathroom so you can puke your guts up before you reach the end of the chapter.

Yes, as you've probably already gathered, the best place for Grot was definitely behind the counter.

And yet all of a sudden, in the blink of an eye, she wasn't.

No, now she was bounding across the length of the café with her arms out wide and a gormless grin on her gruesome face … and there was only one person she was bounding towards!

'If it wasn't for ya, Pinky, I'd still be stuck in Elbow's End,' she cried. 'I owe ya everythin'.'

I tried to back away, but only succeeded in colliding with the door. I had a bad feeling Grot was about to do something I wouldn't like. Something uncomfortably over-friendly. Something sickeningly revolting.

Something like … tripping on a chair leg, staggering forward and kissing me full on the lips.

'Whoops.' Grot took a moment to wipe her mouth across her grubby apron. 'Didn't mean to do that,' she insisted. 'I just wanted to shake ya by the hand.'

So she did. Grot shook it so hard, in fact, that my fingers began to burn and my wrist turned to jelly. Still, anything was better than that kiss.

'Oh, ya've got a bit … on yer face,' remarked Grot, pointing wildly at me.

I reached up and removed something soft and squidgy from just above my lip. On closer inspection, it was long and black and shiny.

And moving.

'That's mine,' said Grot, snatching it from out of my grasp.

I screwed up my face in disgust. 'What is it?'

'A slug,' said Grot matter-of-factly. 'I must've left it behind when I kissed ya. I've been testin' 'em in the kitchen all mornin'. Me and ma Grunt are plannin' on expandin' our ... erm ... *manoo.*'

'Menu?' I said, correcting her.

'Yup, that as well,' nodded Grot. She held up the slug. 'We've been puttin' these little beauties on toast. They're cheaper than beans and they don't crawl off as fast as worms. Maybe you'd like to—'

'Maybe I wouldn't,' I said hastily. 'I'm not hungry. I just popped in to check if you're okay. And you are. I can see that now. The Bulging Bellyful has reopened and you're ... ... you're ... um ... just as I remembered. Which is nice ... for you ... although probably not so nice for everybody else in Crooked Elbow. Still, with that in mind, I think I'll be off. I mean, I wouldn't want to get in the way of all the other customers now, would I?'

'Ah, you crack me up, Pinky.' Grot attempted to punch me playfully on the arm, but something went badly wrong because she almost knocked me over. 'Listen, sit yerself down and I'll bring ya somethin' big and smelly.'

'Like your Grunt?' I muttered.

Grot punched me again, even harder than before. 'So funny,' she sniggered. 'Nah, not ma Grunt, ya wombat. This is another of ma new grubs. I call it ma Bulgin' Bowl of Bits.'

'What is it?' I asked, fearing the worst as I sat down at the nearest table and placed the suitcase between my legs.

'It's a bowl ... with bits in,' replied Grot proudly. 'Lots of bits. Pretty much anythin' bitty that I could lay ma hands on.'

'It sounds absolutely vile,' I blurted out.

'Ya don't know until ya've tried it,' argued Grot. 'What's the worst that can happen? Ya get gut ache … or yer leg falls off … or ya go blind … or—'

'I drop down dead,' I remarked. 'Right here. In your café.'

'Wouldn't be the first time,' shrugged Grot. 'Or the second. Or the third. Not even the twenty-eighth. Let me just go and fetch it for ya, Pinky. Ya might even like it.'

I nodded. I have no idea why. Maybe just to shut her up.

Grot had barely vanished into the kitchen when, to my surprise, the bell jingled and a customer entered the Bulging Bellyful. I turned to look, shocked to find that it was two men. No, scratch that. It was actually one man and his dog. No, double scratch that. It was definitely two men. Hold on. Scratch that for a third time. It was almost certainly … no, it wasn't … oh, this might take some explaining.

One of the men was tall and bedraggled with dirty white hair, patchy stubble and a long, grey coat that reached all the way down to the toecaps of his heavy boots. The other, meanwhile, was walking across the length of the café on all fours like a dog. Yes, you did just read that correctly. He was covered in some kind of hooded cape that concealed both his head and body. A black studded collar, however, was on show around his neck. The collar was attached to a lead. And the lead was being held by the man beside him.

'Good morning, Maggot,' said Grey Coat gruffly. I smiled awkwardly as he guided his human hound to the table next to mine. I was still smiling, in fact, when the bell jingled again and in walked another customer.

No, make that another two customers.

This time it was a man and a woman. The man was wearing a white suit with matching shoes and trilby hat, and a black shirt and tie. There was a white patch over his left eye and a tattoo of a black heart on his opposite cheek. The woman, meanwhile, was dressed in a white wedding dress and chunky black trainers. Her jet-black hair was perfectly straight and brushed forward over her eyes before it came to a sudden halt at the tip of her nose.

'Greetings,' said White Suit, as they made their way hand-in-hand to one of the tables.

I nodded back at him and then quickly turned away. That was when I realised I had company of my own. A woman dressed head-to-toe in camouflage gear had appeared from nowhere and sat down beside me. She was bald on top, whilst her face and much of her head were plastered with mud. She stared back at me when she saw me looking, but that was all. She never spoke. She didn't blink. And there was no chance she was about to crack a smile any time soon.

I can't quite believe what I'm about to write, but the Bulging Bellyful was beginning to fill up with customers. I, for one, didn't like it ... and neither would they when they sampled the food!

The bell jingled again and I was relieved to look anywhere but at my camouflaged companion. The relief soon faded, however, when I spotted who had entered. To my horror, I had run into them already that day.

Run into *and* run away from.

Without breaking stride, Wheezing Wally and Sneezing

Stan marched over to the table behind White Suit and Wedding Dress and sat down. I couldn't tell if they had seen me because of their sunglasses, but this had to be more than just a coincidence. At a guess, they had somehow tracked me here and then followed me inside. But why?

I was about to join the suitcase under the table when Grot burst out of the kitchen. Unsurprisingly, she came to a sudden halt when she saw how things had changed.

'Hey, lover boy,' she hollered, banging on the wall behind her to get Grunt's attention. 'Somethin' strange has happened out 'ere.'

'Just lick it up,' Grunt shouted back. 'No one will notice.'

'It's not that,' yelled Grot. 'I don't do that no more. No, I'm talkin' 'bout humans. Lots of humans. We've got … customers.'

With that, Grot hurried back into the kitchen and slammed the door behind her.

It was only when the walls had stopped shaking that I realised the scruffy man with the grey coat was stood at my table.

'The name's Skinner,' he announced, 'but you can call me Mr Skinner. And this is Mr Bones,' he continued, gesturing towards the human hound knelt down beside him. 'Apologies for the interruption, but there's someone we seek … a boy … and we were hoping you could help us.'

'Perhaps,' I said warily. 'What's his name?'

'The Pink Weasel,' revealed Skinner, studying me closely. 'And, the funny thing is, he looks a lot like you!'

7.'LET THE FUN BEGIN ...'

Mr Bones placed his hands on my table and began to bark.

No, not his hands. His paws. He was a dog, after all. Wasn't he?

I looked around the Bulging Bellyful at the rest of the customers. There were a few curious glances in my direction, but nothing more. Why did nobody else seem to find this strange apart from me?

Mr Skinner hushed his human hound before he spoke again. 'You seem to have gone very quiet, Maggot. Very quiet indeed. Is there something troubling you?'

'Too much to mention,' I muttered under my breath. 'No, if you really want to know I was just trying to picture this Pink Weasel you're searching for. I mean, any boy with a face as handsome as mine wouldn't be so easy to forget now, would they?'

'Ha!' A seemingly unamused Mr Skinner smacked his hand against the side of his leg. To my surprise, it made a strange *clanging* sound. 'Good joke,' he cried. 'Like ho-ho-ho funny. My sides are splitting. Do *you* know the Pink Weasel? *You*? The boy who looks exactly like the Pink—'

'Just Pink Weasel,' I said, butting-in. 'There is no *the*.'

The smile on Mr Skinner's face vanished in an instant. 'Listen, you little troll, we both know who you are so there's no point trying to pretend otherwise. You are the Pink—'

'No, I'm not,' I argued. 'I'm just Pink Weasel. There's a big difference.'

Mr Bones began to growl. He was lurking somewhere under the table and I didn't like it. If I wasn't careful he might start nibbling at my kneecaps.

'There are two ways this can go,' began Skinner, suddenly serious. 'The easy way or the hard way—'

'Or *you* could just go away,' I suggested. 'That's the best of a bad bunch.'

'The easy way,' said Skinner, ignoring me completely, 'is you come quietly. You leave with us now. We walk out of this pigsty together.'

'What's the hard way?' I asked. 'Don't tell me I've got to hang around and eat some of Grot's frighteningly foul food.'

'The hard way is you refuse to leave,' Skinner continued. 'If that happens, things will turn sour. Mr Bones will have to be released for a start. Do you know why I keep him on a lead? It's because he can't be trusted. He's … unpredictable.'

'You mean dangerous,' I said, glancing under the table.

'No, I mean unpredictable,' insisted Skinner. 'He's—'

'Unpredictably dangerous,' I said, butting-in again. 'Or just dangerously unpredictable. A lot like my good self. Okay, so it's one thing to think that I'm this Pink Weasel you seek so badly, but it's another to assume that I'm just going to leave with you. You're a stranger, after all … and that spells danger. Almost. I mean, you do have to change a few letters first, but that shouldn't be too tricky. Not even for a big bruiser like you. And as for your manners ... where do I start? Would it be too much to expect a simple please or thank you? And, no offence intended, but why didn't either you or your furry friend brush your teeth before you left the house this morning? Or wash your hair? Or scrape those crusty bits out from inside your nostrils? Just a few things you might want to consider for next time ... whoa!'

I shielded my face as a raging Mr Skinner raised his fist in anger. When I looked again, however, Skinner's fist was still stuck in mid-air, but now there was another hand gripping hold of it. And that hand belonged to the camouflaged woman sat beside me.

'Do not threaten the child!' she hissed.

Mr Skinner shrugged her off, but then bent forward so the two of them were eyeball-to-eyeball. 'Who are you, lady?'

'Captain Olga Kartoffel,' revealed the woman. She spoke with an accent, her words slow and stilted. 'Maybe you have heard of me.'

'There's no maybe about it,' frowned Skinner. 'I haven't. Sorry to disappoint you.'

'It would be safer for you if you had,' remarked Kartoffel. 'As for the child, I have travelled halfway across the world to find him. And now I have.'

'And so have I,' smirked Skinner.

'Yes, but the child is sat at my table,' Kartoffel insisted, 'therefore he belongs to me.'

'The Maggot is not sat at your table – you're sat at *his*

table!' argued Skinner. He followed that up by poking me in the side of the head. 'I'm right, aren't I? Tell her.'

'I'm not telling her anything,' I muttered.

'My work here is done,' said Kartoffel, standing up. 'Mission accomplished. When the child leaves, he leaves with me.'

'Oh, it's like that, is it?' An infuriated Mr Skinner wagged his finger in the Captain's face. 'What you seem to be forgetting, however, is that you are one and we are two—'

'And we're two as well!'

My gaze shifted to the other side of the café as the curious couple in the corner both rose from their chairs.

'The arguing ends here,' said the man in the white suit. 'You see, whether you like it or not, the kid is coming with us … and there's nothing you can do about it!'

'The kid?' repeated Skinner, confused. 'You mean the Maggot?'

'No, he means the child,' said Captain Kartoffel.

'I think I might be one and the same person,' I chipped in. 'Although I'm not that young. I'm technically a teenager.'

Mr Skinner pressed a finger to my lips. 'Hush your maggot mouth,' he said sternly. 'Let the grown-ups talk. Starting with him,' he said, pointing across the café. 'Who are you?'

'They call me Frankie Fingertips,' revealed White Suit.

Mr Skinner just snorted. 'Big deal. Everybody has fingertips.'

'That's true, but not everybody likes to keep them under their hat,' boasted Frankie, tipping his trilby as he spoke. 'I had thirteen up there last time I counted. One finger from each of my victims. I take the tip once I've finished with them. You know, like a souvenir. Something to remember them by.'

'You've got thirteen mouldy old fingertips hidden under your hat?' I blurted out. 'I wondered why there was a curious smell when you first walked in.'

'Frankie … Frankie,' cried Wedding Dress, pulling on her partner's sleeve. 'Aren't you going to introduce me to your friends?'

"Course I am, Sweet Pea,' nodded Frankie. 'This vision of loveliness is Candy Gloss. She's both sweet and sickly. She's also my gal so hands off.'

'Hey, guys,' said Candy, waving with both hands at the rest of the café. 'It's a real treat to meet y'all but, here's the thing, at some point in the very near future I'm probably going to have to hurt you. *All* of you. It's nothing personal; it's just what I do.'

'Although hopefully not today,' said Frankie swiftly. 'Not if the rest of you fine, fine folk let us stroll right on out of here with the kid tucked safely under our wing.'

'I don't think so,' growled Skinner.

'Not a chance,' insisted Kartoffel.

'In that case,' said Frankie, skipping around the table, 'let the fun begin …'

Mr Skinner yanked on the lead as Mr Bones slipped out from under the table, whilst Captain Kartoffel simply stood up and clenched her fists. I took this as my cue to dive for cover when I heard a loud, crashing sound coming from

THE HUNT FOR HUGO DARE

somewhere behind the counter. Next thing I knew, Grot had burst out of the kitchen. She was weighed down with two large trays, both of which were piled high with bowls.

'Sit down, sit down,' she bellowed. 'There's enough to go around.'

To my surprise, everybody did as they were told. As carefully as she could (not very), Grot then made her way from table to table, placing a bowl or four on each one she passed. Seconds later, the trays were empty.

'Tuck in,' she said, grinning from ear to ear. 'There's more where that came from.'

'I'm sure that won't be necessary,' muttered Skinner.

'What is this stuff?' moaned Frankie, prodding at the contents of the bowl with his finger. 'I think I've seen something similar coming out the back end of a horse.'

'Cheeky,' laughed Grot. 'Nah, this is ma Bulgin' Bowl of Bits. It's just bits … in a bowl. Not too hard to get yer head around. Just call me when ya've finished,' she said, heading back towards the kitchen.

'You'll be waiting a long time,' Skinner remarked.

'Longer than that,' added Candy from somewhere behind her fringe.

The moment Grot had disappeared from view, everybody stood back up again.

No, not everybody.

There was still two more customers who were yet to introduce themselves.

'I don't mean to be the bearer of bad news, but those two goons are pretty keen on me as well,' I said, nodding over at

Wheezing Wally and Sneezing Stan.

'Those two? I thought they were dummies,' frowned Frankie. 'You know, to make this dump look busier than it really is.'

'They may be dummies,' I said, raising an eyebrow, 'but they're dummies with guns.'

Mr Skinner pulled open his coat and gave me a flash of something shiny inside. 'Maggot,' he said with a smirk, 'we've *all* got guns.'

'Now, where were we?' Frankie grabbed Candy by the hand as the two of them edged closer to my table. 'Oh, yeah. Let the fun be—'

'Wait!' I cried. 'Let's do this properly. If it's me you're all after, then it's only fair that I should choose who I go with. Makes sense, right?' I stood up quickly before anyone could disagree. 'Hmm, this is tricky,' I said, peering around the café. 'I don't want to hurt any of your feelings. Rogues and wrong 'uns can be quite sensitive these days—'

'No more!' growled Skinner. 'Your voice … it hurts my brain … just hurry up and—'

'Decide,' I said, finishing his sentence. 'And I have. I choose … you!'

With that, I lifted my hand from the table and pretended to point across the café.

Instead, I grabbed a Bulgin' Bowl of Bits and threw it at the one person who I had a clear shot at.

Just like Frankie Fingertips had predicted, the fun had most certainly begun.

8. 'YOU HAVE MY WORD.'

The Bulgin' Bowl of Bits hit Mr Skinner full in the face.

Nobody really knew what the *bits* were – not even Grot – but they couldn't have been anything pleasant. That was proven to be the case when the bowl fell away and its contents stuck stubbornly to Skinner's features. Long, streaky bits of something nasty were dangling from his nose, whilst much smaller, lumpier chunks of horribleness were sticking to his stubble. I had half-expected Mr Skinner to explode with anger, but he didn't. No, he just stood there, too sickened and too stunned to move. For the time being at least, he was out of action.

One down. Six to go.

Starting with Mr Bones.

I leapt up onto my chair, careful not to get bitten as the human hound jumped at my table. Snapping and snarling repeatedly, his face may have been hidden behind his hood, but I could still make out his teeth. Black and jagged, they were unnaturally sharp and capable of causing all manner of pain given the chance. With that in mind, I chose my foot over my hands and lashed out in self-defence. Now it was

Bones's turn to back away as I kicked him firmly in the side of the head. It didn't take him long, though, to come again. Like it or not, I needed more than a simple shoe to shake off this particular animal-like attacker.

No, what I needed was another Bowl of Bits.

With one eye on the human hound, I searched blindly behind me, but came up empty-handed. Where had all the bowls gone? Surely nobody had made the mistake of trying to eat from them.

Don't be daft, Hugo. Of course they hadn't.

I found this out for certain when Captain Kartoffel flashed into view. Sliding along the floor on her knees, she had a bowl in each hand and her aim set on one particular target.

Thankfully, it wasn't me.

Sensing danger, Mr Bones spun around on all fours, but there was nothing he could do to stop the first bowl from hitting him fair and square in the face, whilst the second landed with a soggy *splat* on top of his hooded head.

Double whammy.

Scrambling to her feet, Captain Kartoffel grabbed me by the elbow. 'It is time to depart, child,' she ordered. 'Do not argue. Arguing will only make things worse. Worse for you.'

Well, when you put it like that …

The Captain was all set to make a run for it when she slipped on something soft and stringy by her feet. Somehow, she kept her balance. 'That was close,' she breathed.

But what happened next was even closer than that.

Not in the least bit hindered by her own ridiculous

fringe, Candy Gloss picked up a bowl and tossed it blindly into the air. I watched as it spun higher, almost to the ceiling, before it began to drop. Not only was it falling fast, but it was also heading straight for me. Without missing a beat, I shuffled slightly to one side, just in time to see the bowl land somewhere else.

And that *somewhere else* was right on Captain Kartoffel.

She cried in horror as the bowl bounced off her shoulder … and then cried some more as its contents spilled all over her. I knew she must have swallowed something *bitty* when she let go of my elbow and fell to the ground, clutching her stomach in agony. For her, the fight was over.

Grot had done it again. And I, for once, was extremely grateful.

I turned suddenly at the sound of another cry. This time it was a cry of joy, however. And it was coming from Candy Gloss. Yes, it had been a good shot, I couldn't deny her that (especially when you consider that Candy couldn't actually see anything). But celebrating in the middle of a battle zone was sure to end in disaster.

And guess what? It did.

Candy's joy came to an abrupt halt when Wheezing Wally crept up behind her and tipped a bowl over her head. Just for a moment the contents stayed where they were, clumped together like a big bitty sandcastle, before gravity kicked in and they began to slide down her fringe. A bewildered Candy just stood there, frozen solid, before it dawned on her what was happening.

Then she screamed.

I covered my ears, although I could easily have closed my eyes. I had seen enough. There were bowls flying left, right and centre and everybody was taking a hit.

Everybody … except me.

Fearful for my own safety, I clambered over the Captain and joined the suitcase under the table. The first thing I did was pull a chair towards me and use it as a barricade. Now I had a good view of everybody from the waist down, but they couldn't see me.

Hiding, though, was only a temporary solution to a very serious problem. With that in mind, I looked beyond the chaos that was playing out in front of me and focussed on the exit. It was at least three table lengths away from where I was knelt. A few seconds to run, but what if I crawled? Ten … eleven … twelve at most. It was a risk, but it was a risk worth taking. I couldn't understand why any of those rotters wanted me so badly, but they did. That was a fact. And there was no way I was about to let that happen.

Okay, twelve seconds. That was definitely doable. And there was no time like the present to definitely do it.

I had barely made my move when something heavy barged into me from behind. Steadying myself, I was all set to kick out in anger when I realised exactly who it was who had joined me under the table.

'Why don't they like ma Grunt's cookin'?' said Grot sadly. There was a tear running down her face. No, my mistake. She wasn't crying at all; she was just sweating. Sweating badly.

'It's got nothing to do with Grunt's cooking,' I replied.

'It's Grunt's cookin' they're all throwin' about,' Grot remarked accurately. She shuffled closer, almost as if she expected me to comfort her in some way or another. I didn't, of course. Yes, she was a friend (kind of), but I still didn't like her anywhere within touching distance of me.

'It's nothing personal,' I insisted. 'The bowls make a pretty good weapon, that's all. I don't know why you brought so many out of the kitchen.'

'I just wanted to make people 'appy,' shrugged Grot.

'Don't waste your time worrying about them,' I blurted out. 'Not when you've got me to worry about. Starting with getting me out of here.'

Grot suddenly looked on the verge of real tears. 'Ya're leavin'?'

'For now,' I replied. 'But I'll return. I promise. I'll come back with a whole cleaning crew and more mops and buckets than you can possibly count.'

'One … two … three then,' said Grot, pleased with herself.

'No, three hundred,' I declared. 'We'll make the Bulging Bellyful look better than ever. That shouldn't be too difficult, of course, but it will have to wait. For now I need your assistance. Do you think you can cover me whilst I make my escape?'

'Cover ya?' Grot pulled a more hideous face than usual. 'What with? A tablecloth? A blanket? Or would ya prefer it if I laid on top of ya and flattened ya like a pancake?'

'Definitely not,' I said hastily. 'I just want you to do everything you can to keep them away from me.' The table shook as someone leapt on top of it. 'They're getting closer,' I whispered. 'Do you think you can help?'

'I reckon so,' nodded Grot. 'Stop them from stoppin' ya. A lot like this …'

Reaching out from under the table, Grot grabbed whoever was standing on it by their ankle and began to pull. It was Frankie Fingertips who eventually came crashing down head first in a crumpled heap. Something else must've got crumpled as well – thirteen *something elses* that he kept under his trilby – but the thought of that was too revolting for me to even contemplate.

'Yes, exactly like that,' I said, grinning at Grot. 'It's goodbye for now, but I'll be back. You have my word.'

And with that, I grabbed a hold of the suitcase and started to crawl towards the door.

Twelve seconds …

I didn't need to see it with my own eyes to know that the chaos that was unfurling behind me was only getting more and more chaotic with every passing second. Tables were being overturned whilst chairs were tossed through the air. There was food everywhere. Well, not exactly food as such.

Nine seconds …

I dodged several broken bowls and scurried between two table legs before I knelt on something green and lumpy. A stain from another day perhaps. Maybe another year.

Six seconds …

I was halfway there.

And that was when I felt it. A sharp pain in the sole of my foot. So sharp, in fact, that I stopped crawling and glanced over my shoulder.

Mr Bones was right behind me, his teeth clenched tight around my shoe. My first reaction was to hit him with the suitcase, but, try as I might, I couldn't swing it hard enough. Bones seemed to realise this and quickly removed both my shoe and sock. Now there was nothing to stop him from taking a proper bite of something far tastier. My toes were the obvious target. I had five of them (no, I'm not showing off), but that still didn't mean I was prepared to lose one.

The breath caught in my throat as the human hound pulled back his head, opened his mouth and … shrieked out loud. I looked beyond his teeth and saw something moving behind him. It was Grot. Somehow, she had crept up unnoticed and done to Mr Bones what he was about to do to me.

She had bitten him.

Bitten him on the bum.

Letting go of my foot, Mr Bones began to roll about on the floor in agony.

I was free.

I refused to look back as I climbed to my feet and raced towards the door. Looking back would only slow me down and that was the last thing I wanted. Yanking on the handle, I scrambled outside and staggered along the pavement. I was minus one shoe, my shorts had ripped along the seam and I was covered head to toe in bits. I smelled bad. Really bad. Like Grot bad. And that was probably as bad as a person could ever smell.

Battered and bruised and barely able to walk, I thought

about where I was heading next. The Impossible Pizza was one option, but I quickly decided against it. No, there was somewhere else I had to be. Somewhere I could drop off this suitcase once and for all.

Let's just hope the wind blows the stink off me before I get there.

9.'NOT NERVOUS, ARE WE?'

I arrived at Smog Suites exactly seventeen minutes and thirty-three seconds after I had escaped from the Bulging Bellyful.

With the suitcase tucked safely under my arm, I tried to blend into the background as I made my way there, but that was easier said than done. It was a Saturday morning and the weekend shoppers were out in force. Cluttering up the paths and pavements like ants in a … um … ant hill, they seemed to be both everywhere I turned and most places I chose to avoid. And just like when I had left Crooked Green earlier that day, every man, woman and child I passed seemed to find me far more interesting than they should have. Call me a paranoid prune (I'd rather you didn't), but I had never had so many suspicious stares and gloomy glares, furious frowns and evil eyeballs, in a single morning. And let's not mention the two pigeons that swooped down on me and almost took my head off. They definitely didn't like me. I could tell that without even asking them.

Back to Smog Suites and the gigantic building that I found myself outside of was an ultra-modern, super-shiny apartment block that seemed to go on and on and on before it eventually disappeared into the clouds. The Big Cheese had informed me that Computer Chip lived at the very top. The thirty-seventh floor. I tried to count from the bottom up, but only reached twenty-two before all the floors seemed to merge together and I could no longer tell where one ended and the next one began.

With no time like the present, I hurried over to a pair of sparkling glass doors and slipped inside before I was spotted out in the open.

'Mickey the Fix has been expecting you.'

I had barely made it through the door when I heard a voice. My instincts told me it was coming from a curved desk to my right, but there was no sign of anybody stood behind it. Nevertheless, I decided to keep my senses on red alert as I crept towards it. I don't do it on purpose, but I had wandered unknowingly into many a trap in my young life … and had no wish to do so again.

And, thankfully, I didn't.

'Not over there – over here!'

I shifted my gaze to the other end of the entrance hall. That was when I saw him. *Him* being a short, stout man with wonky glasses, a lopsided grin, and fiery-red hair with an equally fiery beard. Dressed in baby-blue work overalls with a pencil behind one ear, a screwdriver behind the other and a hammer under his armpit, he was crouching down beside a large sign at the foot of a staircase. Even from a distance I could see *Out of Order* had been painted on the sign in black.

'Mickey knows what you're thinking,' chuckled the man, as I stopped creeping and walked swiftly towards him. 'How can stairs be Out of Order? Well, they can. And now Mickey will tell you why, yes he will, thank you very muchly.'

I waited for him to do as he said. Over thirteen seconds later I was pleased I hadn't held my breath at the same time.

'Not going to believe him, though,' giggled the man eventually. 'You'll think Mickey is all stuff and nonsense. But he's not. No, what Mickey's about to tell you is so shocking it'll make your teeth melt.'

I screwed up my face. Make my teeth melt? That was a new one. And almost certainly impossible.

The man stood up from behind the sign and studied my face a little closer. 'What's up with that mug of yours?' he asked, laughing out loud. 'Mickey's seen more life in a damp sponge.'

'Sorry,' I shrugged. 'I just thought—'

'Never think,' the man butted in. 'Mickey doesn't. Not with his head, anyway. Mickey prefers to think with his hands.'

'Like a handyman?' I guessed.

'Exactly,' grinned the man. 'Mickey's very handy.'

'So, where is he?' I asked, looking over my shoulder. 'This Mickey you keep on speaking about?'

'Mickey's here, Mickey's there, Mickey's every-blooming-where,' sang the man cheerfully. 'And that's because he's me. We are one and the same. Mickey's a fixer. He solves problems.'

'Like those stairs?' I said, pointing at the sign.

'Just like those stairs,' agreed Mickey. 'You won't believe why they're out of order. It's so ghastly it'll make your eyeballs explode.'

Once again, I doubted that would happen.

With a little sideways shuffle, the handyman moved away from the staircase. 'Allow Mickey to introduce you to this fella,' he remarked, gesturing towards the elevator. 'He goes up and down, down and up, and sometimes a bit of both. Never complains, though. Never grumbles. And always does as he's told. So, where would you like him to take you to?'

'The thirty-seventh floor,' I replied. 'Also known as the top.'

Mickey burst out laughing for no apparent reason as the door to the elevator began to open and he stepped forward. 'Don't be shy,' he said, beckoning me inside. 'This is the only way to travel.'

I held my ground. I had been hoping to use the stairs, however high up in the sky Computer Chip's apartment was. Don't ask me why, but I had an unnatural dislike of elevators. I said don't ask me! What's that? Oh, you haven't. Okay. Suit yourself.

'Chop-chop,' said Mickey, urging me to join him. The door began to close, leaving me with no other option but to do as he asked and hop inside. Next thing I knew we were on the move.

1 … 2 … 3 … 4 …

There was an awkward silence that I couldn't let linger for thirty-seven floors. 'You never did tell me what was wrong with the stairs,' I said, making small talk for the sake of it.

'No, Mickey didn't, did he?' Still chuckling under his breath, the handyman removed the hammer from under his armpit and began to delicately stroke it. 'That's because Mickey can't,' he said. 'He can't tell you because there's nothing wrong with the stairs!'

5 … 6 … 7 … 8 …

Oh dear. That didn't sound good. And neither did the noise I made a moment later. Starting in my stomach, it managed to escape from my bottom before I had a chance to stop it.

'Not nervous, are we?' sniggered Mickey.

'A little,' I had to admit. 'If I'm being honest it's been a strange morning.'

'That's a shame,' shrugged the handyman, 'because things are only about to get a whole lot stranger. Starting right now with Mickey's number one problem.'

9 … 10 … 11 … 12 …

I screwed up my face. 'Maybe it's something I can help you with.'

'Maybe so.' Mickey stopped smiling for the first time since we had met. 'It's you,' he said, stone-faced. 'You're the problem … and now Mickey's going to fix you good and proper!'

10.'NO FIXING NECESSARY.'

13 … 14 … 15 … 16 …

The elevator fell silent as it moved smoothly through the floors. I didn't like the sound of that. No, not the silence – I'm talking about Mickey the Fix's final sentence. That *I was the problem and he was going to fix me.* I'm mean, that's wrong on every level. I've known problems and they're nothing like me. And the last time I looked I didn't need fixing either. And even if I did, I certainly wouldn't ask for help from an overly cheerful handyman and his worryingly solid-looking hammer.

And that was why I decided to put Mickey straight before he did something I was sure to regret.

'Consider me a problem-free zone,' I remarked hastily. 'I'm at the top of my game. One hundred-and-fourteen per cent perfect. No fixing necessary.'

'That's not what Mickey's heard,' argued the handyman. The grin had returned, which only seemed to make matters worse. 'You've been making a nuisance of yourself, yes you have, make no mistake. Mickey's here to take you off the streets.'

'I'm perfectly capable of taking myself off the streets,' I insisted. I followed that up by nodding nervously at the hammer. 'What are you planning on doing with that?'

'Mickey's not going to hit you if that's what you mean!' the handyman chuckled. I breathed a sigh of relief before he spoke again. 'No, wait … that's not true. Mickey *is* going to hit you with it. Quite hard as well. So hard it hurts.'

17 … 18 … 19 … 20 …

'Is there anything I can do to change your mind?' I asked desperately.

'Afraid not,' smirked Mickey. Right on cue, he lashed out with the hammer. As the handyman had said, if it had hit me it would've hurt. Fortunately, it didn't.

But it did hit the suitcase. Quick as a flash, I had lifted it in front of my face to block the blow. I half-expected an appalling *crunch* as the hammer struck the laptop, but it never came. That was a stroke of luck. Computer Chip may have been an expert, but I doubted even he could do much with a laptop in two pieces.

21 … 22 … 23 … 24 …

Mickey came again and I did exactly the same thing.

'Stop doing that,' he grumbled.

I took his advice onboard and, with the suitcase out in front of me, charged forward and pushed him back until he collided with the wall behind him. Mickey gasped in pain, but it wasn't enough to stop him from swinging blindly in my direction. Thankfully, the suitcase was too large and he couldn't quite reach around it.

'Not fair,' cried the handyman. 'Just let Mickey hit you!'

'I may be stupid ... but I'm not that stupid!' I replied. No, really. I'm not. But I was struggling. Struggling to keep Mickey the Fix at arm's length.

25 ... 26 ... 27 ... 28 ...

Mickey could see that I was tiring and got ready to swing again. I knew then that I couldn't keep on doing this. Ducking and dodging. Swerving and shifting. Sooner or later I would have to find a way to end things.

I chose sooner.

The hammer was about to come crashing down on me when I swung the suitcase and knocked it clean out of Mickey's hands. Slamming against the side of the elevator, it landed with a horrible *clang* before finally settling in one corner.

'Now who's about to get whacked?' I said, raising the suitcase above my head. 'I'll give you a clue. It's not me.' I paused for effect. 'It's you ... obviously.'

29 ... 30 ... 31 ... 32 ...

The grin vanished from Mickey's face as he dived panic-stricken towards his hammer. He grabbed it with both hands, but that was the easy part. The not-so-easy part was trying to stop himself from crashing head-first into the same corner of the elevator.

Ouch. That looked painful.

Bending down, I poked the handyman twice to see if he moved. Then I prodded him three more times to be certain. I even squeezed his nostrils together, but that was just for fun. Satisfied that he wasn't about to spring up and surprise me any time soon, I gave him a quick once over. By the look of things he had knocked himself out. Shame. That'll teach him to mess with me and my suitcase.

33 … 34 … 35 … 36 … 37.

We had arrived.

There was a loud *ping* as the door slid to one side. Mickey the Fix was still out for the count so I pressed the button marked *G* for Ground Floor and slipped out of the elevator. The doors were already beginning to close when I remembered the suitcase. Hopping back inside, I grabbed it and then got out as quickly as possible. If I had left it a moment later the laptop would've gone the same way as the handyman.

Down to the ground. Never to be seen again (fingers-crossed).

Safe (for the time being at least), I took in my new surroundings. Oddly enough, the thirty-seventh floor was made up of one long corridor and only two doors. Both were closed but neither was numbered, although they did have a tiny plaque just above the handle. A nameplate perhaps. I made my way to the first of the doors and realised that the plaque was engraved. The lettering was so small even an eagle would've complained, but if I squinted hard enough I could just about make sense of it.

EMPTY.

Whether that was the name of the occupant or just the apartment's current state didn't really concern me. It didn't concern because I was already on the move.

I stopped at the second door and pressed my nose to the plaque. It started with a C.

C for *CHIP*.

I was about to knock when the elevator *pinged* behind me. No, that wasn't possible. How could somebody be getting out on the thirty-seventh floor? I had only just sent it to the bottom and there was no way it could've got all the way back to the top again in such a short length of time.

Unless Mickey the Fix had woken up, of course.

Gripping hold of the suitcase, I was all set for another fight with the happy-go-horrible handyman, when the door swung open and two hands grabbed me roughly around the neck. Before I had a chance to object, I was dragged over the threshold and thrown to the floor. The suitcase joined me a moment later before the door slammed shut.

Somehow, without me even asking, I was inside the Computer Chip's apartment.

Now it was time to find out why I couldn't have just been invited in like an ordinary visitor.

11.'DON'T STARE AT THE SCREENS!'

I peeled my face off the floor so I could introduce myself to whoever had dragged me inside.

'Nice to meet you. I'm Pink Weasel, but you can call me—'

A bony hand slapped against my mouth, stopping me mid-sentence. It belonged to a tall, gangly woman in a disgusting brown dressing gown and matching slippers. Her hair was stiff like straw, her face was thin and drawn, and her eyes were bloodshot. She looked exhausted, something I could certainly relate to after everything I'd been through that morning.

'Get down,' she whispered. She removed her hand, but still watched me like a hawk until I did as she asked. Raising herself up onto her tiptoes, she then moved swiftly to secure a bolt at both the top and the bottom of the door before finishing things off with a metal chain just above the handle.

I was about to stand back up again when Thin Face did something unexpected and sat down beside me on the carpet.

'Nice to meet you,' I said, starting from scratch. 'I'm Pink Weasel, but you can call me—'

This time Thin Face pressed a finger to my lips. 'Not so loud, please,' she insisted. 'You wouldn't want them to hear you, would you?'

'I wouldn't want who to hear me?' I shrugged.

'The odd couple, of course,' said Thin Face bizarrely. She pointed towards a spy hole in the centre of the door, perfect for … erm … spying. 'I've been watching them,' she revealed. 'They're probably outside even as we speak. Take a look for yourself if you don't believe me.'

I crawled across the carpet and did as she suggested. The tiny hole didn't provide the best of views, but at least I could see what was going on in the corridor without anybody seeing me.

What I saw was a white trilby hat.

Now, I'm no expert when it comes to unusual headgear, but I was eighty-nine percent certain I had seen that hat before. At the Bulging Bellyful to be precise. Less than an hour ago. I even knew who it belonged to.

Frankie Fingertips.

I was still peeping outside when the man himself turned towards the door. Right beside him was Candy Gloss. For a moment they gazed lovingly at one another before Frankie did something else entirely. Striding forward, he pressed his face up to the spy hole. We should have been eyeball-to-eyeball, but we weren't. No, we were eyeball-to-eye patch.

He couldn't see inside – I was sure of it – but that didn't stop me from edging away from the door as silently as possible.

'I've been studying their movements,' remarked Thin Face, once I'd re-joined her on the carpet. 'They've not been here long, but they keep on coming and going … and then coming and going …. and then coming and—'

'Going?' I guessed.

'How did you know?' said Thin Face. 'I think they must be looking for something.'

'Or someone,' I said, shuffling awkwardly on the spot. 'Which reminds me, I'm here to see Computer Chip.'

'I know,' nodded Thin Face. 'I'm his mum. Mrs Chip.'

His mum? I wasn't expecting that.

'I've brought him this,' I continued, holding up the suitcase.

'I know that too,' repeated Mrs Chip.

'It's got a laptop inside,' I revealed.

'I know that as well,' said Mrs Chip, echoing herself.

'You seem to know a lot,' I said suspiciously.

'Only because the Big Cheese called me,' Mrs Chip confessed. 'He told me to prepare for an incoming arrival. A peculiar little schoolboy to be precise,' she said, casting a weary eye over me. 'But then, as I told the Big Cheese, I'm used to peculiar little schoolboys. Talking of which, shall I take you to my Compy now?'

I screwed up my face. 'Your … Compy?'

'My Computer,' explained Mrs Chip.

'Oh, do you call him that, too?' I asked, surprised. 'I thought it was just a nickname.'

'Well you thought wrong,' said Mrs Chip. 'Computer's a lovely name for a lovely boy. Well, a lovely-ish boy. An occasionally lovely boy. Okay, so he has been lovely before. At least once or twice in his life. Just not for a while.' Mrs Chip stopped for breath. 'Would you like to meet him?'

'You don't make it sound very appealing,' I muttered under my breath.

Mrs Chip, however, didn't appear to hear me as she climbed sluggishly to her feet and set off down the hallway. 'Compy's in his bedroom,' she said. 'He's been stuck in there for some time now so I hope you're not easily offended by revolting smells.'

Mrs Chip stopped at the first door on her left, knocked gently and then slowly dropped the handle. The stench from inside hit me harder than a hippo in a hurricane. A repulsive mix of stinky feet and sweaty cabbage, it took all my powers of nose control not to let go of the suitcase and leg it straight out of the apartment as fast as my one shoe would take me.

Clearly used to the offensive odour, Mrs Chip wandered in without a care in the world. The curtains were drawn and the room would have been dark if it wasn't for the glow from … wait … let me just count them … one hundred and four computer monitors. Okay, so that number might not be entirely accurate, but there were banks of them everywhere I looked. Wall to wall. Ceiling to floor. I was still counting them, in fact, when Mrs Chip threw herself in front of me and covered my eyes.

'Don't stare at the screens!' she cried.

'Why not?' I asked, shrugging her off. 'Is it top secret?'

Mrs Chip shook her head. 'Not that I know of. I just don't like the bright lights and flashing images … they make

your eyes go all fuzzy. Now, where is he? My lovely boy …
he never ventures far … ah, there he is.'

Crouching down, Mrs Chip pointed under one of the
many tables that ran around the outside of the room. It took
me a moment, but I eventually spotted him. Small and
scrawny, he was at least four years younger than me and
about two-thirds my size. His face was deathly pale, his hair
was long and knotty and there were big, dark rings under his
eyes. Sat cross-legged on the carpet, he was hunched over
two keyboards, both of which he appeared to be using at the
same time. I blinked away the glow from the monitors and
realised Chip was wearing nothing but a stained vest
(chocolate, egg and blackcurrant at first glance) and a pair of
lime green underpants (stains unknown).

'You seem surprised,' said Mrs Chip, glancing over at me.

It was true. 'I was expecting someone a little more …
man-like,' I remarked.

'Compy's almost nine-years-old,' stressed Mrs Chip.
'He's a genius and I love him dearly. He can, however, be
quite … quite—'

'Whiffy?' I guessed.

'Volatile,' said Mrs Chip, correcting me. 'Like a human
volcano, ready to erupt at any moment.' With that, she drew
a breath and edged a little closer to her son. 'Compy,' she
said softly. 'Compy … it's me … your mum.'

'He can't hear you,' I said, pointing at his ears. 'He's
wearing headphones.'

'Oh, so he is,' sighed Mrs Chip. 'That's a shame. It means
I'm going to have to touch him. And he doesn't like being

touched. This probably won't end well.'

Mrs Chip reached out with a shaky hand and tapped nervously on her son's shoulder. 'You've got a visitor, Compy,' she whispered.

And that was when Computer Chip exploded.

Not literally. It's not that kind of book. But he did get mad. Very mad. As in *ranting and raving and roaring and raging* mad.

Scrambling out from under the table, the first thing Computer Chip did was pull the headphones off his ears and throw them across the room. 'You scared me, Moo-ma!' he shrieked. 'I don't like it when you creep up on me! Why didn't you warn me?'

A crestfallen Mrs Chip opened her mouth, but the words refused to come.

'She did warn you,' I said, speaking up for her. 'I heard her, even if you didn't.'

Computer Chip stared at me in disgust. 'What … is … this?'

'His name is Pink Weasel,' explained Mrs Chip. 'He works for SICK. The Big Cheese sent him. You like the Big Cheese, don't you, Compy?'

'Not particularly,' replied Computer Chip rudely. 'And I don't like this Weasel thing either. He's weird.'

'*I'm* weird?' I blurted out. 'You're a fine one to talk!'

'He's brought you a laptop,' continued Mrs Chip, trying to calm her son. 'You love a nice laptop, don't you, Compy?'

'Maybe,' said Computer Chip stubbornly. 'What does he want me to do with it, Moo-ma?'

'Turn it on for a start,' I remarked. 'There's information on it that we desperately need. We were hoping you could—'

'Not you!' spat a sullen-faced Computer Chip. 'As far as I'm concerned you don't even exist.'

I glared at the nine-year-old boy in front of me before turning my attention to the suitcase. Given the chance, I could do a lot of damage with that particular piece of luggage. Just ask Mickey the Fix.

'Pass it here then,' demanded Computer Chip, holding out his hands. 'Hurry up. I'm very busy. Give it to me … now!'

'I'll give it to you alright,' I muttered. And I did. Slowly, so not to cause alarm, I passed the suitcase to Computer Chip. What did you expect me to do? I was hardly going to whack him around the head with it, was I? Not today, at least …

Plonking it down on the floor, Computer Chip unzipped the suitcase and clumsily removed the laptop. 'Yes, fairly bog standard … nothing too difficult,' he said smugly. 'I'm prepared to start working on it immediately, but I refuse to do anything whilst the Weasel thing is still in my bedroom.' Computer Chip made a point of spinning around on the spot until he had turned his back on me. 'Just make him go away, Moo-ma,' he whined. 'His face is making my eyes water.'

I gritted my teeth, clenched my fists and … headed straight for the door before I did something I was sure to regret. 'I'll be in the lavatory if anybody needs me,' I announced. 'Just give me a shout when you've finished.'

'It's the last door at the end of the corridor,' said Mrs Chip, smiling weakly at me.

I returned the smile as I exited Computer Chip's bedroom. I thought I had got away, but the last thing I heard was the boy himself.

'Where's my breakfast, Moo-ma? I want my breakfast. Fetch … me … my … breakfast!'

I only stopped moving once the bathroom door was shut firmly behind me. That was better. Now I couldn't hear a thing. Or rather, I couldn't hear Computer Chip. Which was precisely what I wanted. I didn't really need to use the lavatory – I just wanted to get away from that beastly little brat before things took a turn for the worse.

With time to spare, I let my mind wander as I began to pace up and down the seriously limited floor space. If Computer Chip could do half of what the Big Cheese imagined, then there was a good chance I'd leave Smog Suites with enough information to fill a laptop (makes sense, right?) Not only that, but we'd hopefully know more about Deadly De'Ath. He was the priority, after all. If we could track him down and then stick him back where he belonged then Crooked Elbow would be a much safer place for everyone.

Including me.

I was still pacing the floor when an almighty *crash* knocked me right off my stride. I couldn't be certain, but it seemed to be coming from the hallway. Turning towards the door, I was all set to step outside and investigate when the sound of the crash faded, only to be replaced by a flurry of voices.

This wasn't the hideous howl of Computer Chip, though. Nor was it the wary whisper of his Moo-ma (that's mum to me and you.)

No, this was another odd couple altogether.

The oddest couple of all perhaps.

12.'IS THERE A KID IN THAT BEDROOM?'

I held my breath as I gently eased the bathroom door to one side.

The gap I had created was barely wide enough to fit a letter through, but it still gave me a perfectly adequate view of what was going on outside in the hallway.

Or rather, what was going *down*.

The bolts had been broken, the chain had snapped and the door to the apartment had been smashed clean off its hinges. Now it was laid out on the carpet like an over-sized domino. Beyond that, there were two people stood in the doorway. Hand-in-hand and cheek-to-cheek, they continued to chat amongst themselves as if flattening a door was the most natural thing in the world. Which it wasn't, of course. Not for me.

For Frankie Fingertips and Candy Gloss, however, it most probably was.

It seemed that waiting outside the apartment on the off-chance I might appear was no longer enough. No, now they had taken matters into their own hands. And the door had been the one to suffer.

I was still peeking through the gap when a flustered Mrs Chip came bounding out of her son's bedroom. 'What was that?' she cried.

'That was me, madam,' remarked Frankie, stomping all over the door as he entered the apartment. 'Greetings,' he said, tipping his hat. 'You don't know me … and pretty soon you're going to wish that we had never met!'

A somewhat pre-occupied Mrs Chip ignored him completely as she looked down at the carpet. 'My door!' she gasped in disbelief. 'What have you done to my door?'

'Oh, I was hoping you wouldn't notice that,' grinned Frankie. 'Still, no harm done. We had to get in and that was the easiest way to do it. Tell her how it was, sugar plum.'

'My Frankie speaks nothing but the truth,' gushed Candy, jumping up and down on the door.

'You could've just knocked,' Mrs Chip moaned.

A confused Candy stopped and shrugged. 'Why didn't I think of that?'

'I would still have a door if you had,' grumbled Mrs Chip. 'And you two would be outside. Where you should be.'

Frankie just shook his head. 'Leaving us waiting on your doorstep isn't a possibility I'm afraid,' he remarked. 'We think you might be hiding someone that we're particularly keen to get our—'

'Breakfast!'

I couldn't see him, but I'd recognise Computer Chip's whining warble anywhere.

'Did you hear that?' asked Frankie, raising an eyebrow at his partner.

'Sure did,' said Candy from somewhere behind her fringe. 'I heard it … and I didn't like it.'

'Madam, I'll only ask you once.' Frankie pointed along the hallway. 'Is there a kid in that bedroom?'

'No,' said Mrs Chip hastily.

'Am I hearing you correctly?' Frankie blurted out. 'Did you really just say *no*? Because that's not true, is it? I *know* there's a kid in there. And I want you to bring him to me. Bring him now.' Frankie paused. 'Or else …'

'Or else what?' gulped Mrs Chip.

'Or else things are going to get ugly,' added Candy, wagging her finger.

'They're ugly enough already,' mumbled Mrs Chip. She squeezed her hands together to stop them from shaking. 'I can't bring you what doesn't exist.'

'Why do you keep on saying that?' cried Frankie. 'Don't make me go in there and drag him out myself!'

'No, make *me* do it, Turtle Dove!' An over-excited Candy began to clap her hands together. 'Let me … let me … let me,' she sang over and over again.

'Be my guest,' said Frankie. Candy took this as her cue to skip along the hallway. Mrs Chip reached out in despair and tried to grab her, but it was too little too late. One push later and Candy had simply swept her to one side before she entered Computer Chip's bedroom.

Tiptoeing away from the door, I took a moment to consider my options. Frankie was blocking the only exit and

I didn't fancy my chances of either racing past him unnoticed or fighting my way out of there. And what if I did manage to? I could hardly leave Mrs Chip and her beloved Compy to fend for themselves, could I? Okay, maybe Compy, but not his mum.

A high-pitched scream drew me back to the door. When I looked again, Candy was leaving the bedroom. Her steps were small and her hands were full.

Full of Computer Chip.

Yes, he had joined her in the hallway, but I doubted it was through choice. Not unless his preferred way to travel was upside down.

'Looks like you've caught yourself a little fishy,' laughed Frankie.

'He's a wriggly tiddler alright,' agreed Candy, holding Chip up by his ankles. 'And do you know what happens when a tiddler keeps on wriggling? They fall right off the hook!'

'No! Don't drop him!' cried a panic-stricken Mrs Chip.

'Yes, drop me,' Computer Chip demanded. 'I want you to put me down this instant.'

'You want me to put you down?' echoed Candy, barely able to contain herself. 'But that's what I want, too.'

'Don't,' begged Mrs Chip. 'He'll get hurt.'

'Will he? In that case …' A determined Candy lifted Computer Chip as high as she possibly could and then let go. I thought about looking away before he hit the carpet, before deciding that even I deserved a treat from time to time.

Worst luck, Computer Chip landed with less of a *splat* and more of a *bump*. Nowhere near painful enough for my liking.

'This isn't the kid we're looking for,' remarked Frankie. 'And yet I'm pretty sure the kid we *do* want is somewhere here in your apartment. Tell me I'm wrong and we'll leave you be.'

'You're wrong,' said Mrs Chip firmly.

'You're right,' argued Computer Chip. 'There was a boy here. A Weasel thing.'

I began to tense up. If only Candy would do me a favour and drop him once again. And this time off the roof.

'I, however, sent him away,' continued Computer Chip smugly. 'That was an absolute age ago. He must've gone by now. But he did leave a laptop behind.'

'A laptop?' repeated Frankie.

'I've only just started looking at it,' revealed Computer Chip. 'Would you like to me to go and fetch it for you?'

Frankie took a moment before shaking his head. 'I'm only interested in the kid,' he declared. 'Maybe one of us should take a look around, though,' he said, turning towards his partner in crime. 'Just to be on the safe side.'

'And maybe that one of us is me,' replied Candy, moving swiftly along the hallway. 'I love a good game of hide and seek.'

I shuffled away from the door, more on edge than ever. There were a number of other rooms she would arrive at first, but it wouldn't take her long to reach the bathroom. I needed to get out of there. That was obvious. How I was going to do it, though, was another matter altogether.

First things first, I looked around for any available escape routes. There was a window. Good start. I tried to push it open, but it only shifted an inch or two before it jammed. At best, I could just about squeeze my arm through. The rest of my body, unfortunately, wasn't quite so squeezable.

I switched my attention to the toilet. Lifting the lid, I leant forward and peered inside, disappointed to find that it was no bigger than every other toilet I had ever come across. Still, needs must I suppose. Yes, it was a tight fit, and I didn't really fancy getting wet, but here goes nothing …

I was about to climb in feet-first when I glanced over at the bath tub. There was a shower curtain pushed against one side. If I pulled it all the way along the rail then it would stretch the length of the entire bath. And that got me thinking. It wasn't a great hiding place. It wasn't even a *good* hiding place. But it was still a hiding place. And that meant it was better than nothing.

The shower curtain was white in colour with various swirls and squiggles splattered all over it. Crouching down by the taps in the bath, I gently pulled it across until I was completely concealed. There. I had done it. No turning back now.

I had almost got comfortable when I heard Frankie's voice coming from the hallway. 'Any joy, Baby Cheeks?'

'Not really,' replied Candy sullenly. 'I've only got one room left. The bathroom. Wish me luck …'

With that, the door flew open, making the shower curtain billow in the breeze.

'Is he in there?' called out Frankie.

'Not that I can see,' Candy shouted back. 'It's too small to hide a kid. I think we're wasting our time.'

My heart was fluttering like a butterfly on a treadmill. I was almost in the clear. I had dodged them.

'Unless …' I could see the outline of Candy Gloss as she stopped suddenly and stared at the bath. 'You don't think …' she muttered to herself. 'No, surely not. Nobody would be that stupid.'

I watched as her fingers wrapped around the shower curtain.

I had spoken too soon.

I hadn't dodged them at all. And I wasn't in the clear. Not in the slightest.

What did Candy say about being that stupid?

13.'THE SPY YOU'VE NEVER SEEN.'

The sparkly polish that Candy Gloss had painted on her fingernails was starting to crack.

A lot like my nerves, in fact.

Any moment now she would pull back the shower curtain and then what? She would definitely see me – that was inevitable – so there was no way I could pretend otherwise. Not even if I managed to squeeze down the plughole and escape through the sewers (note to reader – that's not going to happen. So don't even think about it.)

No, my only option was to go on the offensive. As soon as Candy opened the curtain I would pounce. She wouldn't be expecting it and I would have the advantage. I could knock her down and keep on moving. Straight over the flattened door and past Frankie. If everything went to plan, I could be out of the apartment in a matter of seconds. Mrs Chip and Compy would have to fend for themselves, I'm afraid. Sorry about that.

I readied myself for what was to come. I was Hugo Dare. Codename Pink Weasel. Agent Minus Thirty-Five. If anybody could do this, it was me.

My confidence slipped the moment the curtain began to slide along the rail. Whether I liked it or not, it was time to pounce.

And I was about to do just that when Frankie called out from the hallway.

'You're right, Melon Balls. The kid's no longer here. We'll pick him up somewhere on the streets so there's no need to fret.' Frankie paused. It lasted for less than a second, but it felt like forever. 'I'll buy you a cookie if you promise to come quietly,' he said.

'A cookie?' Candy let go of the shower curtain. 'You'll buy me a cookie, Honey Pie?' she squealed. 'Make it two and you've got yourself a deal.'

'I'll make it two dozen, Fairy Wings,' laughed Frankie. 'Now, let's beat it before we outstay our welcome. Judging by all this mess, there's a whole lot of cleaning to be getting on with. And that door's going to need fixing sooner rather than later. They don't want no strangers wandering in uninvited, do they?'

A giggling Candy skipped out of the bathroom and joined her partner in the hallway.

'If you see that kid again be sure to call me,' said Frankie. I could only guess that he was talking to Mrs Chip. 'Just scream my name out the window and I'll be sure to come running. It's Frankie Fingertips in case you're wondering. And don't you forget it!'

'I won't … I promise … not a chance … no way,' spluttered Mrs Chip.

'Well, I'm not in the least bit interested in that Weasel

thing,' muttered Compy. 'But I am interested in those cookies. Buy me one … now!' he demanded rudely.

'I'll buy you a cookie if you find me the kid,' remarked Frankie.

And those were the last words he uttered. I heard footsteps over the flattened door and more giggling before both eventually faded to nothing. Convinced that Frankie and Candy had finally left for good, I stood up and got ready to draw back the shower curtain when somebody beat me to it.

'They've gone,' panted Mrs Chip. Not only were her hands shaking uncontrollably, but she kept on glancing nervously over her shoulder in case the two rogues decided to return. 'You're dripping,' she said, looking me up and down. 'From head to toe. You haven't actually had a shower, have you?'

'Not that I can remember,' I said, wiping my brow as I climbed out of the bath tub. 'It's just sweat. Things got pretty tense in there.'

'Things got pretty tense out here as well,' said Mrs Chip, breathing heavily. 'I was absolutely petrified. Who are they anyway? And why are they so desperate to get their hands on you?'

I followed Mrs Chip out of the bathroom before I spoke. 'I know their names, but nothing else,' I admitted. 'I've no idea who they are, and I haven't got a clue what they want with me. I'll find out, though, I'm sure. One way or another, I'll get to the bottom of this.'

'You!' Computer Chip spun around on his heels and shot

me an accusing finger as I passed his bedroom. 'You're still here!' he shrieked. 'I should go and tell Frankie Fingertips so I can get that cookie—'

I raced forward and took him out at the ankles before he had a chance to leave the apartment. 'You're not going anywhere,' I said, pinning him to the carpet.

'Moo-ma!' Computer Chip cried. 'Get the Weasel thing off me!'

'You've work to do,' I continued. 'That laptop needs … um … laptopping.'

'Moo-ma!' Computer Chip cried again. 'The Weasel thing keeps telling me what to do.'

'And as for me.' I took a moment to think about what I was going to say next. 'I'm not really here,' I remarked. 'I'm the spy you've never seen. Do you understand?'

'Moo-ma!' cried Computer Chip for a third time.

'Oh, Compy,' sighed Mrs Chip, shaking her head at her son. 'For once in your life, will you please just do as you're told?'

With a face like thunder, Computer Chip scowled at both his mum and me before he slouched off to his bedroom, stopping only to slam the door shut behind him.

Mrs Chip swallowed. 'I should've said that years ago.'

'Better late than never,' I replied. 'Talking of which, I think it's time I left you to it.'

'I agree,' nodded Mrs Chip. 'Wholeheartedly. Take care and disappear. Go somewhere you can't be found … oh, you seem to have forgotten something!'

Mrs Chip hurried back into her son's bedroom before

returning with the tatty old suitcase. If I'm being honest I had been hoping to leave it behind. Still, another hour or two carrying it around would hardly make a difference, would it?

With the suitcase by my side, I bid Mrs Chip a fond farewell as I stomped all over the flattened door. One sneaky peek later and I was pleased to see that there was no sign of Frankie and Candy (or even Mickey the Fix for that matter) in the corridor. With nothing or no one to stop me, I left the apartment behind and hurried towards the elevator.

Think again, Hugo.

I spun away at the last moment and opted for the stairs instead. I doubted they were *Out of Order* like Mickey had insisted. That was just a trick. A trick to trap me. Wise to his ways, I took to the top step whilst preparing myself for the challenge that was to come.

Thirty-seven floors was a long way up. And a long way up meant it would take a long time to reach the bottom.

This might take a while.

I'll meet you when I get there.

Like I had imagined, there was absolutely nothing wrong with the stairs. Except that they were all so very stair-like. And there was lots of them. Over five hundred, in fact. Maybe one thousand. I don't know. I stopped counting at forty-one so I can't really be certain.

I pushed past the *Out of Order* sign and continued along the empty entrance hall before exiting Smog Suites a moment later. Once outside, I stayed close to the walls as I made my way from building to building. I couldn't stay hidden forever, but it was a start.

My destination was the SICK Bucket. It would take about seventeen and a half minutes to get there at walking pace. Seventeen if I was nervous. And I was. Nervous, I mean. And who could blame me?

I moved into the open and tried to pick up speed. For the first few minutes everything went to plan and there was nothing for me to worry about.

And then there was.

I heard a noise high in the sky and shifted into the shadows for fear of being spotted. I watched as it emerged from out of the clouds and realised it was a helicopter. That was unusual. It wasn't often you saw a helicopter in Crooked Elbow. Especially one that seemed to be circling close to where I was.

It took a while but the helicopter eventually disappeared, leaving me free to set off again. The SICK Bucket wasn't that far away now. If I could get there in one piece I'd be as happy as a pig in a puddle. Then I could tell the Big Cheese about everything that had happened. Like Mrs Chip had said, maybe I should go into hiding for a while. Both out of sight and out of reach. Off grid. As long as there was plenty of food available I'd be fine. Nothing too fancy. Chocolate … pizza … chocolate pizza. The thought of it was enough to make my stomach rumble.

It rumbled so loud, in fact, that I failed to hear the car that was creeping up behind me.

14.'GOOD THINGS ALWAYS COME TO THOSE WHO WAIT.'

The car wasn't a car.

It was actually a bright yellow pick-up truck. Big and loud and ugly, it was the kind of thing I shouldn't have been able to ignore.

And yet, somehow, I had.

The first I knew about it, in fact, was when it slowed to a crawl beside me and the door swung open. I had barely turned to look before I was dragged into the vehicle. The door slammed shut behind me and I was trapped. The whole thing had taken less than three seconds. Two at most.

Two seconds for the pick-up to pick me up off the street.

'Greetings,' said Frankie Fingertips. With only the empty suitcase separating us on the back seat, he leant forwards and rested a hand on my knee. 'I knew we'd catch up with you eventually and here we are. Good things always come to those who wait.' Frankie paused as the pick-up jerked without warning. 'If I was you I'd think about strapping myself in,' he suggested. 'I'm not trying to scare you, but this could be one heck of a bumpy ride.'

'I heard that!' cried Candy from the driver's seat. 'I'm not that bad. I'm not that good either, but, hey, who's complaining?'

Candy took her hands off the steering wheel as she glanced over her shoulder and smiled. I didn't smile back. Instead, I snatched at my seatbelt. To my horror, Candy's fringe was still covering her eyes. She was driving blind and blindly driving. A dangerous combination if ever there was one.

My theory was proven correct as the pick-up veered wildly from side to side before it bumped against the kerb. I tried to hold on tight, but there wasn't much to hold on to. Only myself. And I wasn't that easy to get a grip of. Not when I was shaking so much.

'Candy may be my gal, but I shouldn't really let her drive,' said Frankie, raising an eyebrow at me. 'She's never passed her test.'

'I've never even had a lesson,' laughed Candy. 'I just get in and … *zoom!* I don't know why, but I seem to find it really, really … whoa!'

The pick-up juddered as Candy mounted the pavement. We were about to hit a street lamp when she spun the steering wheel in desperation and we bounced back into the road. I was scared before, but this had taken it to a different level altogether. Now I was absolutely petrified.

'Having fun?' Frankie grinned.

'What do you think?' I cried out. 'This is crazy. And so is Candy!'

'Yes, she is, isn't she?' agreed Frankie. 'That's what I love most about her. Which reminds me …' Frankie edged closer until the rim of his trilby was poking me in the side of the face. 'You don't think much of me, do you, kid?'

I didn't reply. How could I? Not when my jaw was clenched tight with fear.

'Candy thinks it's her that you don't like,' continued Frankie, 'but that's not true. It's me. I can see it in your eyes. You think I'm a little strange. And that's why you keep on running away from me!'

I was about to speak when Candy put her foot down on the accelerator. The engine roared and the truck shot forward, throwing me back against my seat. The speedometer shuddered as it flickered past fifty … sixty … seventy miles per hour. We were travelling far too fast for a built-up area. Dangerously fast, in fact.

'We could've been friends,' sighed Frankie. 'Hey, maybe there's still time,' he said, perking up a little. 'Let's play a game. Why don't you try and guess what's under my eye patch?'

'Why are you doing this?' I blurted out. 'What do you want with me?'

'No, I asked first,' grumbled Frankie. 'Play the game. It's only fair. What's under my patch?'

I shook my head, distracted. 'I don't know … nothing … just an empty socket—'

'Wrong!' Frankie lifted the patch and revealed another eye. Another perfectly normal, blinking and winking eye. 'Good trick, eh?' he said, grinning from ear to ear.

'Not really,' I mumbled. 'Now it's my turn to ask a

question. What do you want with me?'

'*I* don't want anything with you, kid,' revealed Frankie. 'That's the truth. No word of a lie. I couldn't care less about who you are or what you've done. Somebody, however, clearly cares a lot.'

The speedometer flickered past seventy-five … eighty … ninety miles per hour.

'I'm what you'd call a hired hand,' confessed Frankie. 'A mercenary. And so, too, is Candy. We work for money. Big money. Expertise like ours comes at a high price.'

In the blink of an eye, all the buildings on either side of us disappeared, only to be replaced by tall, over-hanging trees and dense woodland. I knew where we were. Cutter's Wood. Right on the tip of Crooked Elbow, it was a long way from the SICK Bucket and even further away from home.

'It's nothing personal, kid,' shrugged Frankie. 'I've got no problem with you. It's just that you're valuable. Practically priceless. A human treasure chest.'

The speedometer touched one hundred miles per hour. The pick-up was shaking and so was I. We couldn't carry on like this for much longer. Because if we did, there would only be one outcome.

Crash … bang … wallop.

Frankie rubbed his hands together. 'I'm sure we'll be well rewarded when we finally hand you over to … what in the wild, wild world is that?'

I followed Frankie's gaze and spotted something up ahead. It was in the middle of the road, hovering slightly off the ground.

Surely not.

It couldn't be.

No way.

'Look out!' cried Frankie.

Candy stamped on the brakes, but the pick-up was going far too fast to just grind to a sudden halt. Instead, it swerved and skidded. It jumped and jolted. And then it began to spin. Round and round and round. If ever there was a time to throw up, it was now.

But I was far too scared to be sick. I was too scared to do anything, in fact. Anything except wait.

Wait for the pick-up to stop spinning … and then hope I was still alive when it did so!

15. 'THIS IS MY FIRST TIME.'

It took a while, but the pick-up finally skidded to a halt.

I waited until everything had settled before I dared to open my eyes. The first thing I should've seen was Frankie Fingertips sat beside me in the back of the vehicle.

I should've ... but I didn't.

He was no longer there. His door was swinging open, though, which got me thinking. Had he been thrown out of the vehicle, leaving him dazed and confused in a heap by the roadside? Possibly. Was he now unconscious? Perhaps. Dead? Probably not if I'm being honest. Still, fingers crossed ...

I didn't mean that, of course. Well, not much. Just a little.

With Frankie nowhere to be seen, I released my seatbelt and leant forward for a closer look at Candy Gloss. Sat rigid in her seat, her eyes were wide and unblinking, whilst her fingers were clasped tight around the steering wheel. I poked her in the cheek, but she didn't even flinch. Her skin was cold, though, almost as if she had frozen solid with shock.

With no one to stop me, I grabbed the empty suitcase

and clambered out of the pick-up. My legs felt like jelly and my head was turning cartwheels, but both were hardly worth complaining about after everything that had happened. Instead, I switched my attention to what had caused the pick-up to swerve and spin in the first place. It had surprised me the moment I first saw it … and it still surprised me now.

But then who wouldn't be surprised at the sight of a helicopter in the middle of the road.

I had seen it already that day, hovering above me at Smog Suites, dipping in and out of the clouds, but I had never expected it to land. With both its main rotor and tail rotor still … erm … rotating, however, I figured it wouldn't be long before it took off again.

But not until it had got what it had come for.

I was still gazing in disbelief when a large, shadowy figure climbed out of the cockpit. Dressed head-to-toe in black, he kept his head up and his shoulders straight as he began to stride towards me. In the end it was the sunglasses that gave him away.

The man who had exited the helicopter was Sneezing Stan.

Or Wheezing Wally.

How was I to know? Even close up they looked identical, let alone from a distance. It was only when the goon pressed a handkerchief to his nose and sneezed loudly that I knew I had guessed correctly. It was Stan. Which meant it had to be Wally who was sat upright in the pilot's seat, puffing on his inhaler. I hadn't seen either of them since the food fight at the Bulging Bellyful and – no offence intended – I had been hoping that was the last time I ever would.

Sneezing Stan was halfway between the helicopter and the pick-up when he came to a sudden halt. I tensed up as his hand slipped inside his jacket, fearful that he was about to draw his weapon. With nothing but the suitcase at my disposal, I was all set to use it as a shield when a curious groaning sound drew my attention. I shifted to one side for a closer look and that was when I saw him. Stretched out in the road. Struggling to push himself up.

Frankie Fingertips.

Not only was he the reason that Stan had stopped, but he was also a massive reminder that the next move I made was the most important move I would make that day (until the next move, of course. And then every other move after that most probably.)

Whether I liked it or not, I was stuck between a rock and a hard place. Or just two faceless goons and the oddest couple in Crooked Elbow. Either way, I had three choices. One was Frankie and Candy, and the other was Stan and Wally? Yes, I know that's only two, but the third – making a run for it – didn't really bear contemplating. Let's not fool ourselves; I wouldn't get far. Not on foot. And definitely not with a pick-up and a helicopter hot on my heels.

Two choices.

Let's start with the facts. Both pairings were armed and dangerous, but Frankie and Candy were something else entirely. They were creepy. Disturbingly so. Admittedly, Stan and Wally were a bit creepy too, but the worst they did was sneeze and wheeze and refuse to talk to me. Which, all things considered, was nowhere near as troubling as the fingers Frankie kept under his trilby or Candy's ridiculous fringe.

And that was why I hurried towards the helicopter as fast as my one shoe would take me.

I didn't need to look back to know that Frankie was doing more than just stirring now. Candy must have snapped out of her trance, too, because all of a sudden I could hear them both talking. Which soon turned to shouting. Which then turned to … nothing.

I was so close to the helicopter that all I could hear was the deafening *chuff-chuff-chuff* of its rotors. Sneezing Stan let me pass and I tossed the suitcase in first before diving face-first into the helicopter. Stan followed close behind, stopping only to give Wally a gentle nod. The helicopter had already started to rise as I strapped myself in. I took a deep breath and tried to control my stomach as we swayed from side to side. I knew that looking down at the ground below would only make me feel worse, but I did it anyway. Frankie and Candy were stood directly beneath us, peering up at the sky, waving their fists in anger. It didn't take long before they began to shrink in size. It was too early to say if I had made the right decision in leaving them behind. Not unless I planned on jumping out, of course (which I didn't).

'This is my first time,' I shouted, struggling to make myself heard above the rotors. 'Do you do much … um … *coptering*?'

Sneezing Stan ignored me completely, choosing instead to crack his knuckles as he sat in silence.

'Okay, have it your way,' I sighed. 'If that's what you want, then that's what you'll get. I'll just sit here and keep it zipped. I don't have to speak. I can do lots of other things.' I began to tap my foot to prove it. Then the other foot. Then I clicked my teeth. And picked my fingernails. And rolled my neck. And … no, it was unbearable. I had to say something.

'It's quite fun I suppose, this coptering malarkey,' I blurted out. 'Although I wouldn't want to fall out by accident. Or, worse still, get thrown out on purpose!' I stopped talking as a horrible thought suddenly dawned on me. 'You're not going to throw me out, are you?' I asked nervously.

Sneezing Stan refused to reply. He did, however, grab me by the neck and squeeze.

'That doesn't really answer my question,' I gasped. The helicopter started its descent before I could speak again. To my relief, Stan released his grip and sat back down in his seat. Able to breathe again, I forced myself to peer down at the ground beneath us. The closer we got, the more I could make out. Stretching as far as the eye could see were a series of large open fields. They were all oddly shaped with grass that was greener than green and the occasional over-sized sandpit dotted around in random places.

Hang on. Isn't that a …?

I looked again and realised we were about to land in the middle of a golf course. That explained the sandpits. They were called bunkers. They were used as traps for golfers to avoid. Okay, so I didn't actually know any of that at the time, but I do now. And, trust me, I'll never forget it …

With the ground fast approaching, I closed my eyes, gripped hold of my seat and waited for the moment we touched down. It never seemed to arrive so I gave in to the urge and took a sneaky peek outside. Remarkably, we had landed and Stan had already climbed out of the helicopter. With the suitcase at my side, I quickly joined him on solid ground … and couldn't believe the sight that greeted me.

They were all identical in size – big – and appearance – dressed in black with sunglasses. I did a quick head count and reached eighteen. And that didn't include Sneezing Stan and Wheezing Wally.

Which made a grand total of twenty faceless goons.

Curiously, they had formed a tight ring around a golf cart. That's a tiny vehicle to you and me (and anybody else who happens to be reading over your shoulder). Designed to carry two golfers and their equipment around a golf course, this cart was currently only carrying one. A man.

And what a man he was!

With his flushed cheeks, blond, wavy hair and enormous bloated belly, he was instantly recognisable. Like an exact opposite of the goons that surrounded him, he wore clothes that were so colourful they made your eyes water. I'm talking a vivid pink V-neck jumper, yellow and green checked trousers and dazzling white gloves that refused to be dimmed by the gloomy Crooked sky. Yes, he was dressed for golf, but he was also ready for the circus. Not that anybody would ever dare tell him that. Not to his face, anyway.

Oh … except me.

The golfer climbed out of the cart and looked me straight in the eye. 'Ah, I see we have company,' he bellowed.

I watched as he marched over to the thirteenth tee. I had never met him before, but I had seen him lots of times. On television. Online. In newspapers and magazines. On billboards and banners. Even on sausages. He was everywhere I looked and most places I didn't.

His name was Victor Smog.

He was a powerful businessman and, arguably, the richest man in Crooked Elbow.

All of which got me thinking.

What could a man like that possibly want with someone like me?

16. 'JUST WHACK IT!'

Stood on the tee of the thirteenth hole, Victor Smog lifted his golf club and swung.

I followed the ball as it soared high into the sky before it eventually disappeared from view.

'Nice,' cheered Smog, waving the club above his head in celebration. 'Tell me, you Smogolytes. Don't hold back or spare my feelings. Just hit me with the truth.' He stopped to puff out his chest. 'Stick your hands in the air if I'm the best golfer you've ever seen,' he said smugly.

Twenty pairs of hands immediately shot up into the sky.

Twenty pairs of hands belonging to twenty faceless goons.

'And the cleverest?' added Smog.

The hands didn't drop.

Victor Smog began to grin. 'And the most handsome? And the funniest? And – let's not beat about the bush, people – the most perfect specimen of humanity known to mankind?'

The hands stayed exactly where they were.

'That's what I'm talking about,' whooped Smog. 'The

best just got better. Hey, you Smogolytes, relax a little. We all know how great I am so quit going on about it all the time. Oh, silly me. I almost forgot.' Smog spun around on his heels and flashed me what he probably imagined was a winning smile. 'Welcome to Sweet Smog Valley, bud. The finest golf course in the whole of Crooked Elbow.'

'Or just the only golf course in the whole of Crooked Elbow,' I replied.

'And therefore the finest,' agreed Smog. 'Tell me I'm wrong. Go on. You can't, can you? Because I'm not. I'm never wrong. I've been making right decisions all my life. From day one. I'm what you call a born winner. Hey, where did I leave my manners?' With that, Smog removed a glove before strutting over to me with his hand out-stretched. 'Put it there, bud,' he said. 'I'm Victor Smog … but I'm guessing you already know that.'

It irritated me immensely, but he was right. Of course I knew who he was. Everybody did.

'This must be an absolute thrill for you,' continued Smog, refusing to lower his hand. 'It's not every day you get to meet one of your heroes.'

I screwed up my face.

'Don't look like that,' said Smog, pulling a face of his own. 'It's kinda' ugly. And I don't like to surround myself with ugly people. Now, are you going to shake my hand or not?'

'Not,' I replied stubbornly.

Except that wasn't true because a moment later Sneezing Stan picked me up by my elbows and carried me to his boss.

I was so close now that a handshake was unavoidable. To my horror, Smog's palm was incredibly soft and slippery. Almost inhuman, in fact. Like an eel.

'Why have you kidnapped me?' I asked, coming straight to the point.

'Kidnapped?' Victor Smog started to laugh. It was uncomfortably loud and more than a little bit forced. 'I haven't kidnapped you,' he declared. 'Ask my Smogolytes. I've not left this golf course all day. Besides, the way I hear it nobody forced you to get in my helicopter.'

'I didn't really have a choice,' I moaned. 'It was the best of a bad bunch.'

'I bet,' nodded Smog. 'You are Hugo Dare, right? Pink Weasel? The smallest spy in Crooked Elbow? Don't answer that because I already know. And the fact that you're here, with me, right now, makes me the champion. The all-conquering hero. Victor the victor. Yeh, I like the sound of that.' Victor Smog paused for breath. Unfortunately, he didn't pause for long. 'Don't you get it, bud? I'm the winner. Hey, why am I not even surprised?'

'The winner?' I frowned at Smog as he hopped from toe to toe whilst twirling the golf club above his head. If this was his celebration dance it was quite frankly embarrassing. 'What have you won?'

'I've won the tournament,' grinned Smog. 'The Hunt for Hugo Dare.'

I screwed up my face again. None of this made any sense.

'I told you not to do that,' grumbled Smog, shaking his head at me. To my surprise, his hair fell forward as he did so and completely covered his eyes. Smog moved quickly and put it back into place, but the whole episode got me thinking.

'If I didn't know better I'd say that's a wig you're wearing.'

That was the first thought that crossed my mind. And that was where the thought was supposed to stay. In my head. Never to be spoken out loud. And yet nobody remembered to tell my mouth that. Because somehow – and don't ask me how because this has got nothing to do with me – I shouted it out loud at the top of my voice.

'Did you just say what I think you said?' The golf course fell deathly silent as Victor Smog fixed me with a steely glare. 'Explain yourself, bud.'

'I didn't … I wasn't … I couldn't … I shouldn't …' As far as mumbling goes, that was up there with my best. 'I was talking to myself,' I said honestly. 'And you lot just happened to listen in.'

'This is all my own hair,' insisted Smog, using the golf club to point at his head. 'This isn't a wig.'

'I never said it was,' I shrugged.

'Yes, you did,' growled Smog. 'I heard you. And my ears – just like the rest of me – are never wrong! How dare you come here, to my golf course, and insult me like that!'

'Oh, I don't mind leaving,' I said, perking up a little. 'Just point me in the right direction and I'll—'

'That's not going to happen,' snapped Smog. Without warning, he turned away, took a deep breath or three and then turned back with a broad grin spread across his lips. 'Have you ever played golf?' he asked innocently.

I was about to say *no*, but then quickly changed my mind in case I offended Smog for a second time. 'Yes, I play all the time,' I said instead. 'Morning, noon and night … and every hour in between. I love it loads. I'm gaga about golf—'

'Too much, bud!' said Smog, interrupting me mid-flow. 'I've had an idea, and – just like all my others – it's a good one. You've insulted me and the only way you can make things right is by accepting my challenge. Do you accept?'

'You'll have to tell me what it is first,' I replied.

'It's me versus you in a battle of skill and strength,' grinned Smog, prodding me in the chest with his club. 'I challenge you to a shoot off!'

'A shoot off!' I ducked down and covered my head with both hands. 'I'm not sure I like the sound of that.'

'It's just golf – not guns,' explained Smog. 'A one ball shoot off. Whoever hits the ball furthest is the winner.'

Okay. That didn't sound so bad. Except …

'What's in it for me?' I wondered.

'Good question.' Victor Smog began to tap the side of his head, careful to avoid his hair in case it slipped for a second time. 'Let me see … if you win … no, don't laugh, you Smogolytes, this is serious … if you win, I'll let you go, bud. You can leave right now and that'll be the end of it. Goodbye and good riddance. When you lose, however, I'll hand you over and pick up my prize. Hey, it's nothing personal – it's just business. Sounds fun, right?'

'Yeah, great fun,' I grumbled. 'Given the choice, I can't think of anything else I'd rather be doing.'

'Pleased to hear it,' said Smog. 'Right, there's no time like the present. Prepare to lose, bud ... because that's what's going to happen!'

I looked on in despair as Smog placed a golf ball on the tee and lined up his shot. Lifting the club behind his head, he held it for a moment and then swung. Unfortunately for me, he struck the ball firmly and it flew through the air. I tried to follow it along the fairway, but gave up almost immediately.

'Wow! How far was that?' roared Smog, staring into the distance.

'Too far,' I muttered.

'Exactly,' said Smog, passing me the golf club. 'Your turn.'

I dropped the suitcase and picked up a ball, placing it gently on the tee.

'Good luck,' smirked Smog. 'You're going to need a miracle to beat that.'

He was right. I couldn't hit the ball as far as he had. That was a fact. I knew it. He knew it. We all knew it. So, what could I do? I strained my brain for a solution. There was a way out of everything so there had to be a way out of this.

'Hurry up,' demanded Smog. 'We haven't got all day. Just whack it!'

Just whack it.

Of course. It was obvious really. Why didn't I think of that before?

Stepping back, I lined up my shot and swung the club with as much force as I could muster.

Unlike Smog, however, I wasn't aiming for distance.

No, I was just aiming for Smog.

17.'CAN YOU TEACH ME HOW TO DO THAT?'

I hit the ball.

And the ball hit Victor Smog.

Right between the legs.

Ouch!

I can't really describe what I felt as Smog collapsed in a heap, but I did know what Smog felt.

And that was pain.

And lots of it.

Let's get one thing straight. I hadn't really expected the ball to hit him. Honestly. I'm not that good a shot. No, I was actually intending for it to be more of a distraction. Something to shift the attention away from me. And it had. Kind of.

It was only when the twenty faceless goons gathered around to check that Smog was alright, however, that I realised that this was much, much more than just a mere distraction. This was a chance to escape. To get out of there.

And the best way to do that was parked right beside me.

No, not the helicopter. I'm not completely crazy. I'm talking about the golf cart.

Without thinking (do I ever), I grabbed the suitcase and clambered into the driver's seat. As luck would have it, the key had been left in the ignition. I turned it, expecting the engine to spark into life.

It didn't.

Unsure what to do next, I ducked under the steering wheel and spotted a single pedal where the driver's feet would normally rest. Without thinking (not again), I pressed down on it with my hand and the cart jerked forward. The shock of it was enough to make me let go and the cart ground to an immediate halt.

Ah, that made sense.

Sitting up, I gripped the steering wheel with both hands and stamped down on the pedal, this time with my foot. The cart shot forward in a straight line along the fairway. I couldn't quite believe it, but my escape plan was actually working. I was leaving Smog and his twenty faceless goons behind.

Just not very quickly.

I started to rock back and forth in my seat, urging the cart to speed up, but nothing I did appeared to work. That was when I spotted a speedometer to the left of the steering wheel. It was flickering between ten and fifteen miles per hour. Not a patch on the pick-up truck. Still, at least I knew how fast I was travelling now.

Not very.

Peering over my shoulder, I half-expected to see that at

least one of the faceless goons had set off after me, but I was wrong. They hadn't shifted in the slightest, although several had gone as far as to remove their sunglasses in amazement.

And then there was Victor Smog. He was back on his feet, albeit hunched over with a pained expression on his face. What came out of his mouth next, however, was unexpected to say the least.

'You're looking the wrong way, bud!'

It took me a moment to figure out what he meant. Then I swivelled around in my seat and realised my mistake. I had been so pre-occupied with Smog and his Smogolytes that I had forgotten to steer the golf cart. I had just let it drift where it wanted.

And where *it* wanted was the one place that all golfers tried to avoid.

I lifted my foot off the pedal and tried to spin the steering wheel, but it was too little too late. The cart was already trundling over the lip of the bunker. It was about to crash … and there was nothing I could do about it!

Okay, so the cart may have been a goner, but that didn't mean I had to go the same way. Releasing the steering wheel, I pushed the suitcase out first before following it myself. The sand softened my fall. The cart, meanwhile, balanced for a moment on its front tyres before toppling over onto its roof. I felt bad for about a second. And then a second after that I remembered it belonged to Victor Smog.

Safe (for the time being at least), I crawled under the lip of the bunker so I could catch my breath. I couldn't stay there for long, though. At some point I would have to make my move. But where could I go?

'I know where you are, bud!' shouted Smog. 'You can't hide from me forever.'

Okay, so maybe I'd have to make my move a little sooner than I hoped.

'You hit a ball at me!' Smog continued. 'You ... hit a ball ... at me! Well, now it's your turn to feel pain ... but I'm not going to stop at just one ball!'

I was about to call out and offer some kind of apology when something small and white whizzed over the top of the bunker, missing my head by a matter of inches. I ducked down as it dawned on me what was happening.

Victor Smog was firing golf balls.

And he was firing them at me.

I stayed low as, one by one, the balls either landed in the bunker beside me, or zipped along the fairway, far too close for comfort.

'Nearly ... but not quite,' laughed Smog, as the balls continued to rain down on me from above. 'This is going to really hurt when I eventually hit you, bud.'

Yeah, I had figured that out for myself. I could picture Smog now as he pulled back his club ... followed through with his swing ... and ...

Crack.

Wait. That wasn't the sound of club on ball. That was ... that was ... that was a gunshot!

To my horror, Victor Smog had swapped his golf club for something much more dangerous.

I waited for him to fire again, but the shot never came.

There was no sound at all, in fact. Just silence. Considering Smog was so keen to shout at me whenever the chance arose, it seemed odd that the golf course had gone so eerily quiet. Whether I liked it or not (I didn't, of course), I had to take a peek over the lip of the bunker so I could find out what was going on.

Lifting my head, I let my eyes drift towards the thirteenth tee. Smog was nowhere to be seen. His Smogolytes, however, were just where I had left them, albeit laid on top of one another on the grass. I pitied the poor goon who found himself at the bottom of that particular pile.

Another gunshot sent me scurrying back under the lip.

And that was when two thoughts suddenly struck me.

One, it wasn't Victor Smog or any of his Smogolytes that were doing the firing.

And two, there was only one place that Smog himself could be … and that was at the bottom of that pile. It was obvious really. When the first shot had sounded his goons must have dived on top of him. Those were probably Smog's instructions. To protect him at all cost. Whoops. I bet he regretted that now.

So, if it wasn't Victor Smog that was blasting bullets around the golf course, who was it?

I scanned my surroundings for any sign of movement. At first I saw nothing but open fairway lined with tall trees, before my eyes wandered into the rough. That was an area of the golf course where the grass had been left to grow deliberately. And that was where I spotted a bald, egg-shaped head with a dirty face dipping in and out of sight.

I had seen that face before. Back at the Bulging Bellyful. Sat at my table, in fact.

It belonged to Captain Olga Kartoffel. The camouflage-wearing, mud-splattered soldier.

Like the others, she seemed prepared to do anything to get her hands on me. And that included shooting at Victor Smog!

The captain saw me looking and gestured for me to join her. I screwed up my face. I had been here before. No, not hidden in a bunker; I mean faced with a tough decision. I was still weighing up her offer when I turned back towards Smog. One by one, the goons were beginning to climb off him. Soon he would be back on his feet, angrier than ever. Then the balls would start to come again. Two at once probably. Or maybe he'd just throw the golf club at me.

With that in mind, I clambered out of the bunker and set off for Captain Kartoffel. Worst case scenario, Smog would see me, but at least I was a moving target now. Harder to hit. Especially if I used the suitcase as a shield.

Several seconds later and I thought I had made it all the way to the rough without being spotted.

Guess what? I thought wrong.

'Get after him!' cried Smog. 'Don't let him escape!'

That was the cue for all but two of Smog's Smogolytes to do as they were told and jump into action. Sneezing Stan and Wheezing Wally, however, hurried over to the helicopter and got ready to take off.

I was about to dive for cover on the exact same spot as I had seen Captain Kartoffel when I realised she wasn't there anymore. Already on the move, she was making her way down the side of a slope that ran along the side of the fairway. I kept on moving and saw that the slope led to some kind of valley before it eventually rose and formed another slope on the other side. That explained the name of the golf course. Sweet Smog Valley. The sweet bit, however, wasn't so easy to figure out.

I wanted to shout, but kept it to a loud whisper. 'Wait for me.'

'No,' said Kartoffel bluntly. 'You must keep up.'

'I'm trying,' I moaned.

'Try harder,' Kartoffel demanded.

I did as she asked and picked up my pace as I hurried down the slope. There were trees at the bottom that seemed like a natural hiding place.

'Stop panting,' remarked Kartoffel, the moment I drew level with her.

'I can't help it,' I said, panting more than ever.

'And stop talking,' Kartoffel added. 'They will hear you. And then they will find *us*. And watch where you tread. The ground can be quite boggy down here in the valley. Almost swamp-like. If you get stuck you will never get out.'

I kept my mouth shut and my eyes glued to my feet as I carried on towards the trees. I was almost there when I heard an all too familiar whirring sound coming from the sky. It was the helicopter. Not only that, but the Smogolytes were already stumbling down the slope. Closing in with every step, if they couldn't see us now, they would almost certainly see us soon.

Captain Kartoffel stopped without warning and crouched down. It was only when I joined her in the undergrowth that I noticed she was empty-handed.

'Where's the gun?' I asked.

'What gun?' frowned Kartoffel.

'*The* gun.' It wasn't the best explanation so I tried again. 'The gun you used to shoot at Victor Smog. You fired it twice. I heard it with my own ears.'

'You think you heard it,' argued Kartoffel, 'but you were mistaken. There is no gun. I do not carry weapons. I only use these …'

I flinched as Kartoffel made a sudden movement. Thankfully, she had no intention of hurting me in any way imaginable and chose, instead, to cup her hands together, place them to her mouth and blow. The sound that rang out around the valley was loud enough to scare the birds from the trees and send the Smogolytes scurrying for cover. It was also identical to a gunshot.

A gunshot with no gun.

'That's a neat trick,' I said. 'Can you teach me to do that?'

'Of course I cannot,' snapped Kartoffel. 'This is not the time for teaching. This is the time for disappearing.'

A single Smogolyte drew my attention before I could ask her what she meant. Moving ahead of the others, he was almost upon us.

'I like the sound of disappearing,' I whispered. 'Feel free to tell me exactly how we do that, won't you?'

I waited for an answer, but it never came. Turning back, I soon realised why.

True to her word, Captain Olga Kartoffel had done the unthinkable.

Just like that, as if by magic, she had disappeared.

18. 'SHRINKING OR SINKING?'

With Captain Kartoffel nowhere to be seen, I was all set to weave between the trees in a bid for freedom when I felt something firm grip hold of my ankle.

I glanced down, shocked to find it was a camouflaged hand.

'To disappear completely you must become one with nature,' remarked Kartoffel from somewhere beneath the earth.

I screwed up my face. 'I'm not going to turn into a worm if that's what you mean?'

'No, but you could always behave like one,' explained Kartoffel. 'Follow my lead. Lay down on the ground and cover yourself with anything you can find. Leaves, twigs, dirt, it does not matter. After that, you do not move. Not even an inch. If we are lucky they will not see us—'

'And if we're unlucky?' I wondered.

'If we are unlucky you will get caught,' remarked Kartoffel.

'*We'll* get caught,' I said, gathering up as much of the loose undergrowth as I could manage.

'No, *you* will get caught,' insisted Kartoffel. 'I was right first time.'

I didn't like the sound of that, but tried not to dwell on it as I started to bury myself beneath everything I had collected. My arms and legs weren't that difficult to cover. My head, however, was something else entirely. I don't know why, but hiding my own face in the ground was much harder than I imagined. As a last resort, I smeared dirt across my forehead before resting my cheek on the grassy pillow beneath me. I thought about closing my eyes, but decided instead to leave them slightly open so I could see what was going on.

'He is coming,' warned Kartoffel.

He. Not *they.* By the sound of things there was still only one Smogolyte heading towards us. One was still one, though. And that was a whole lot worse than none.

I listened carefully and picked out the clumsy stomp of the single Smogolyte as he hurried through the undergrowth. Whether he knew it or not, he had found our location. But he hadn't found us.

Not yet anyway.

I laid still. The stomping had come to a halt, only to be replaced by the gentle rustle of leaves and the occasional snapping twig. The Smogolyte was moving slowly now, approaching with caution, nervous about what could pop up at any moment.

Don't panic, Hugo.

He couldn't see me. I was sure of it. I was completely hidden.

But something else wasn't.

The suitcase.

It was so close I could touch it. So that was what I tried to do. Slipping my hand out of its hiding place, I reached for the handle. I had almost grabbed it when I felt something heavy press down on my forearm. It was a black leather shoe.

A black leather shoe belonging to the Smogolyte.

I held my breath and tried desperately to swallow back the scream that had risen from the pit of my stomach. The pain was beyond words. Oh, what's that? You'd like me to try anyway? Let me see. Unbearable. Yes, that sums it up nicely. Absolutely, without a shadow of a doubt, the most unbearable pain I had ever experienced.

That all changed, however, when the Smogolyte shifted his weight and the pain increased tenfold. No, make that eleven-fold. I didn't even know pain like that existed.

With my arm on the brink of snapping like the twigs that surrounded it, the scream that I had failed to swallow rolled over my tongue and pushed against my teeth. It wanted to escape and there was nothing I could do to stop it.

My teeth parted … my mouth opened … and the Smogolyte finally shuffled forward.

The need to scream began to fade as the pressure slowly eased. Instead, I wriggled my fingers, relieved to find that I could still move them. The Smogolyte took another step and I knew I had to act quickly. He still hadn't spotted the suitcase. And he wouldn't do. Not if I moved it out of the way. Carefully, so not to make a sound, I took hold of the handle and began to slide it towards me. The leaves crunched and crackled under its weight. As noises went, you could barely make it out above the whir of the helicopter. The Smogolyte, however, had heard something. And something was enough to make him spin around on the spot.

The first thing he should've seen was the suitcase. And the second was my hand. And the third would've been the rest of me as he dragged me out of the undergrowth.

And yet, somehow, he didn't. Instead, he peered up the slope towards the golf course at the sound of a voice in the distance. A voice he both recognised and obeyed.

'Keep searching, you Smogolytes,' hollered Victor Smog from the thirteenth tee. 'I won't be happy until you've found that pesky spy!'

With the threat ringing in his ears, the Smogolyte hurried back up the slope without a second's delay. I started to count to ten in case he turned back, but gave up at seven when I stuck my head out of the undergrowth. Phew. That went better than I expected. I was about to give myself a pat on the back when I remembered I still had company. And she wasn't that friendly.

'Go,' ordered Captain Kartoffel, crawling out from under her hiding place. Snatching the suitcase up off the ground, I hurried to keep up with her as she moved swiftly between the trees. We were heading deeper into the valley. I took a look behind me, but there was no one on our tail. Wherever the Smogolytes were searching for me, it wasn't here. The helicopter had gone, too. Yes, I could still hear it, but it was no longer hovering overhead.

'Do not move!' said Kartoffel, without warning.

I ignored that last bit and walked straight into the back of her. 'Make up your mind,' I muttered. Whatever she had seen had certainly spooked her. So, what was it? Another Smogolyte perhaps? Two Smogolytes? Or three? Or … oh, you get the picture.

I stopped wondering what it could be when I noticed there was a lot less of Captain Olga Kartoffel than there had been a moment ago.

'You seem to be getting smaller,' I remarked. 'I'm guessing it could be one of two things. You're either shrinking or sinking?'

'Sinking,' replied Kartoffel. 'Do you remember the swamps I told you about?'

'I do now,' I said honestly. I followed that up with a sigh of relief. That could have been me down there, up to my kneecaps in mud.

No, not kneecaps. Kartoffel was up to her waist now.

No, her armpits.

No, her neck.

The captain was sinking fast. I half-expected her to vanish under the surface completely when she came to a sudden halt.

'I have reached the bottom,' she mumbled, barely able to keep her chin out of the swamp. 'One wrong move, however, and I could go under.'

Slowly, so not to disturb the muddy sludge that surrounded her, Kartoffel lifted an arm and reached out towards me.

'Pass me that suitcase,' she ordered. 'Then you can pull me to safety.'

I was all set to do as she demanded when a thought crossed my mind. 'What did you say you were going to do with me when we get out of here?'

'I didn't,' frowned Kartoffel. 'But, just so you know, I am going to swap you for my prize.'

'Yeah, that's pretty much what Victor Smog said, too.' With that, I began to walk away.

'Where are you going, child?' hissed Captain Kartoffel, thrashing about in the swamp. 'You cannot just leave me here.'

'I can … and I will,' I replied. And I did. I ignored her shouts and screams as I made my way through the trees and up the opposite slope to the one we had earlier descended. When I got to the top I found myself on the other side of the golf course. The fifth hole to be precise. As far as I could tell, there was nobody in sight. No Smogolytes rushing along the fairway, or helicopters tracking me from the sky. I couldn't even hear Victor Smog himself, barking orders. As for Captain Kartoffel, I could only guess that she was still up to her eyeballs in sludge. Which left me with nowhere to go and nobody to take me there.

I was free.

But I was also tired beyond belief. Like extraordinarily exhausted. From the moment I had first met Brooke Keeper, the day had taken a turn for the worse and then never recovered. Now I needed to find somewhere to rest and relax. Refuel and recuperate. And, thankfully, I knew just the place.

It starts with an *h* and ends in *ome.*

I'll give you until the next page to figure it out.

19.'WHERE DID MY EYEBROWS GO?'

Home.

That was my destination of choice. I did practically spell it out for you. And, yes, I do realise it's hardly the most imaginative of hiding places, but it was the best I could come up with at short notice.

Allow me to fill in any gaps in your memory. Thirteen Everyday Avenue was a simple house in a simple street surrounded by other simple houses owned by lots and lots of very simple people. Including the Simples themselves. They lived across the road with two goldfish. That was probably the most interesting thing about them.

Back to number thirteen and it was dark by the time I entered through the front door, took off my one and only shoe and padded slowly into the kitchen.

'Nice day, dear?'

My mother, Doreen Dare, was stood at the sink, washing dishes. Well, that was what her left hand was doing. Her right hand, meanwhile, was ironing my father's underpants (with an iron, of course. She didn't just use her palm). Not only that, but there was a paintbrush behind her ear (which she was painting the wall with), a duster strapped to her head (which she was using to remove the cobwebs from the ceiling), and a cloth wrapped around her left foot (which she swiped furiously across the floor as if she was kicking a football).

'What are you doing?' I asked.

'Everything, dear,' grumbled Doreen. 'Always everything. And the only way to do everything is to do it all at once. Still, I'm not one to complain. Never have been, never will be. I just get on with it … every last bit of it … whilst your father … that useless lump of a man I chose to marry … messes about making … and I can't believe I'm about to say this … messes about making exploding toothpaste!'

'Exploding toothpaste?' I repeated. 'Wow! That sounds cool.'

'Of course it does,' muttered Doreen. 'Far more interesting than cooking and cleaning and washing and ironing and dusting and cleaning and—'

'You've already said cleaning,' I pointed out. At the time, I thought I was being helpful. In hindsight, maybe not.

Doreen snorted through both nostrils before dipping her brush into the paint pot. 'Nice day, dear?' she asked again.

It didn't take long for me to think of an answer. 'Definitely not, Doreen.'

'That's good, dear,' said my mother vacantly. 'Just don't call me Dor—'

'It's probably one of the worst days I've ever had,' I continued.

'Pleased to hear it,' said my mother. 'But I'd rather you didn't call me Dor—'

'It's a miracle I'm still alive,' I blurted out.

'That's wonderful news, dear,' said my mother, 'but I still don't want you to call me Dor—'

'Where would you like me to start?' I moaned. 'I've been chased and shot at on Crooked Green … caught up in a food fight at the Bulging Bellyful … attacked by a human hound. Don't ask; you wouldn't believe me even if I told you. Where was I? Oh, yes … hammered by a handyman … saved by a shower curtain … spun around in an out of control pick-up truck … taken hostage in a helicopter … crashed a golf cart before being bombarded with balls … and then almost swallowed up by a swamp. I think that's about it. No, wait. I've also lost a shoe.'

'You've lost a shoe?' Doreen stopped what she was doing – *everything* she was doing – and gave me a hard stare. 'How did you lose a shoe?'

I screwed up my face. 'Didn't you hear what I just said? The loss of a single shoe was the least of my worries.'

'That's easy for you to say,' argued Doreen. 'Shoes are very expensive these days, dear. They don't grow on trees.'

'No, but money does,' I replied smartly. 'Listen, Doreen, the shoe isn't a problem. I'll just go around in bare feet if I have to. Or walk on my hands. I've got skills, remember. Sometimes I think you forget I'm a spy.'

'I never forget you're a dimwit,' muttered Doreen under her breath. She followed that particular remark up by pointing out of the window. 'Why don't you go and see your father, dear? I'm sure he'll be pleased to see you. I banished him to the garden when he set fire to our bedroom curtains with his … exploding toothpaste.'

'Yeah, I think I'll do that,' I said. 'This has been nice, though, hasn't it, Doreen? You and me … catching up … hanging out together. We should probably do it again some time.'

'As you wish, dear,' frowned my mother. 'Just don't call me—'

'Doreen, the pleasure has been all mine,' I said, halfway out the door. 'You know where I am if you need me. Until we meet again …'

As expected, I found my father crouched down in the middle of the garden. Not only was Dirk Dare the tea boy in the SICK Bucket, but he also made things. Things that other people would never dare to dream of.

Things like exploding toothpaste for example.

Striding across the grass, I had almost reached my father when he turned sharply, swung out a leg and tripped me up.

'Why would you do that?' I moaned.

'A good spy should be ready at all times,' Dirk insisted. 'And you weren't. That's your lesson for today, Pink Weasel.'

'You don't have to keep calling me that,' I said, picking myself up off the damp grass. 'Not at home.'

'Once a codename, always a codename,' remarked Dirk bizarrely. 'It's always best to … blimey, what's happened to you? You're a complete mess. Anyone would think you'd spent the day being chased and shot at and attacked and spun around and flown away and ... let me think ... bombarded with balls. Did I miss anything out?'

'That's ... incredible,' I gasped. 'Were you there?'

'No, I just heard you tell your mother,' explained Dirk. 'Don't worry about her. She doesn't understand what it's like to be a spy. I, however ... well, I don't understand either, but I'm trying. I really am.'

Peering over my father's shoulder, I spotted a rug laid out on the grass beside him. On it were four tubes of toothpaste, a jug of water and what worryingly looked like several sticks of dynamite. Several *empty* sticks of dynamite that were now minus their contents.

'It's not easy doing this on my hands and knees,' said Dirk, turning back towards his invention. 'It's a very delicate operation. One wrong move and I'll probably burn the house down.'

'You've already set fire to the curtains,' I reminded him.

'Yes, that's what I told your mother,' whispered Dirk. 'Luckily for me, however, she doesn't know about the four cushions, two blankets and rug I destroyed earlier in the week. Still, you can't make an omelette without cracking a few eggs, can you? Should I test it again?'

'Probably not,' I said hastily.

'You're right,' agreed Dirk. 'Although *probably* not isn't *definitely* not, so I think ... yes, I will test it again. If at first you don't succeed and all that nonsense. Get ready, Pink Weasel. This could blow your nose off.'

I edged away from my father as he picked up the tube of toothpaste in one hand and dangled it over the water.

'It's hard to put into words,' began Dirk, 'but if this goes to plan, then the second the toothpaste touches the liquid, there should be some kind of a reaction. That'll be followed by a massive … ooh, butter fingers!'

Dirk stopped mid-sentence as he accidentally let go of the tube and it landed in the jug. A split-second later there was an ear-splitting boom. The last thing I saw before I dived for cover was a flash of light and a huge plume of smoke as my father was thrown to one side. For a moment I just laid there, my heart punching a hole in my school blazer as I tried to catch my breath. By the time I had sat up, however, my father was already on his feet, bouncing around the garden as he punched the air in celebration.

'It works,' he cried. 'It actually works. This is wonderful. Extraordinary. Absolutely fabulous.' He stopped suddenly and lifted his hands to his face. 'Where did my eyebrows go?'

I was about to tell him when I was beaten to it by my mother.

'Dirk … Dirk … was that you?' she screamed from somewhere within the house.

'No, not me, my love,' mumbled Dirk awkwardly. 'It was … erm … next door's cats. They were … um … setting off fireworks. Totally inexcusable behaviour if you ask me. I'll pop around in a minute and have a word.' My father waited a moment and then winked at me. 'I think I got away with that one,' he whispered. 'Maybe I should call it a night though. No more experimenting today.'

'Can I have a tube?' I asked, pointing towards the toothpaste. 'I think it'll come in handy.'

126

Dirk screwed up his face. 'Not really,' he replied. 'They are quite dangerous. And it's not as if I've tested them properly. They're still in the trial and error phase—'

'I don't just want a tube – I *need* it,' I blurted out. I don't know where that came from or even how it had escaped from my mouth, but it was too late to suck it back in now. 'A lot of strange stuff has happened today,' I admitted. 'Too much for it to all be one big coincidence. I tried to tell the Big Cheese that earlier, but he didn't seem to take me seriously.'

Dirk bit down on his lip, deep in thought. 'Okay, you can have a tube,' he sighed. 'And why don't you sleep in the house tonight? If the threat is real then you'd better take precautions.'

Sleep in the house.

I glanced over at my shedroom. That's a shed-cum-bedroom for those of you who aren't aware of the concept. It was where I spent most of my free time. Through choice, I might add. And that was why I felt reluctant to turn my back on it that evening.

'Thanks, but no thanks,' I replied.

'Suit yourself,' said Dirk, as he gathered his bits up off the rug. 'Just don't use that toothpaste. Not even a blob of it. It'll knock your teeth out if you do.'

I gave him a double thumbs up and then disappeared into my shedroom. It was a tight squeeze, but I was used to it by now. Barely breaking stride, I swerved around two empty plant pots, the lawnmower and half a bag of compost before I finally collapsed onto my bed. Ah, that was better.

It had been a long day. With my eyelids already

beginning to droop, I tried to plan out the next morning before I fell asleep by accident. First things first, I would go and see the Big Cheese. It wouldn't be easy to explain, but both Victor Smog and Captain Olga Kartoffel had mentioned some kind of tournament with a prize going to the winner. The tournament seemed to involve catching me, but I had no idea why. Yes, I worked for SICK, but I was only Agent Minus Thirty-Five. I was hardly at the top of the tree. And yet, all of a sudden, I was the most wanted spy in Crooked Elbow. Everybody wanted a piece of me. And it was what they were planning on doing with those pieces that worried me the most.

Tomorrow, however, would have to wait. With my eyes shut and my brain switched off, there was no shifting me now.

Don't worry; I'll see you soon. Not too soon, mind. The last thing I want is you waking me up in the middle of the night.

20.'I KNOW YOU'RE NOT ASLEEP.'

Good news.

Turns out you didn't wake me up at all … but something did.

Or rather, someone.

It was just gone midnight when I heard a noise outside my shedroom. It was the sound of footsteps. Soft, shuffling footsteps. The kind you only hear when some rogue or wrong 'un is trying to creep up on you.

Anybody else would've been shaking like a lettuce leaf by now, but then I'm not just anybody else. I'm more of a *somebody* else. A somebody else who just happens to be a spy. And as we know, dear reader, spies are always well prepared.

Call me a nervous ninny, but I always take three precautionary steps before I turn in at the end of the day.

Step one – I go to bed fully-clothed. Or, to put it another way, I don't bother to change out of the clothes I was wearing the day before. I even keep my shoes on. Not today, of course, because I had left one behind at the Bulging Bellyful, but normally. Normally being when I haven't been attacked by a savage human hound like Mr Bones.

Step two – I keep three weapons hidden under my bed. At that very moment there was a rolling pin, a broken chair leg and an egg whisk hidden away there. In hindsight, maybe the egg whisk wasn't such a good choice. One of my mother's favourite ornamental vases from the house would've been better. Or even a spade or a rake. Both of those were in the corner of my shedroom, well within grabbing distance. Why had I never thought of using them before?

And step three – I make a point of never actually sleeping. Well, not properly anyway. I'm what you'd call a light sleeper. No, I don't sleep with the light on; it means I wake at the slightest of sounds. The faintest of rustles. The gentlest of footsteps.

A lot like the ones that were right outside my shedroom.

I reached under the bed and snatched the rolling pin up off the floorboards. There was no point just lying there waiting for Tiptoes to come and get me. No, if I moved swiftly I could get to them first. Counter their intended surprise attack with a surprise of my own. With that in mind, I held my breath, steadied my nerves and charged out of my shedroom.

It was dark. Obviously. It was the middle of the night, after all. That didn't stop me, however, from swinging wildly in every possible direction. If Tiptoes had been within range they would have felt the full force of my rolling pin right where it hurts. Unfortunately, they weren't … so they didn't. I stopped swinging and listened instead. There was a slight breeze and the occasional owl, but that was all.

Meaning that, as far as I could tell, there was no one lurking in my garden.

Satisfied that the threat of danger was nothing more than my imagination, I hurried back inside, closed the shedroom door behind me and jumped into bed. This time I kept the rolling pin by my side, though. Just in case.

There. I was safe now. Nothing to worry about. Which also meant that there was nothing to stop me from going back to sleep (except I didn't, of course. Because I don't. Sleep, I mean. I've already told you that. I just rest for a while. With my eyes closed. And my mouth open.)

And that was when I heard it. One … two … three more times. Tiptoes was back. Closer than ever. *Right outside my shedroom* close, in fact.

There was an uncomfortable shudder as Tiptoes pushed against the door. With nowhere to hide, I instinctively pulled my covers up to my chin and pretended to close my eyes as the door began to open. Okay, this was more like it. If I couldn't catch them, then I would fool them into thinking that they had caught me. I would wait … and wait … and wait … until I could sense them beside me and then … wham!

Game over.

I listened carefully, but heard nothing beyond my own breathing. A few seconds later and I started to wonder if I had been mistaken again. Maybe nobody had entered the shedroom at all and it was just the wind. Or my father. Or even my father's wind. Yes, that was definitely something that Dirk was capable of. Creeping about in the dark. Trying to scare me. I suppose it could even have been Doreen, although I couldn't recall the last time she had tried to clean my shedroom after midnight.

I was about to open my eyes when someone whispered in my ear.

'I know you're not asleep.' Tiptoes was a woman. 'Open your eyes.'

Open my eyes? No way. Not in a million years.

'This isn't a game,' the woman insisted. 'We have to go.'

That's what she thinks.

'Oh, please!' The woman was practically shouting now. 'If we stay here any longer we'll both suffer a horrible, gory death!'

I flinched. Only slightly. But it was enough to give me away.

'I thought that might do the trick,' the woman laughed. 'Right, let's move, shall we?'

So that was what I did.

I moved.

Throwing my cover to one side, I grabbed the rolling pin and leapt up onto my bed. I followed the voice and saw Tiptoes for the first time. Dressed in grey, she was short in size and round in shape with bobbed black hair, big eyes hidden behind a pair of thick spectacles and an unnaturally wide mouth.

I knew who it was … but there was nothing I could do to stop myself from swinging the rolling pin straight at her.

Thankfully, I missed.

The momentum, however, was enough to send me

tumbling off my bed. I sat up quickly and cast my eye over my shedroom. To my surprise, Tiptoes had vanished. She hadn't gone far, though. Just to one corner. Hidden behind the suitcase.

'It's me,' she cried. 'Poppy. Poppy Wildheart.'

I kept the rolling pin raised as I edged towards her. Yes, she was the Big Cheese's new personal assistant, but that didn't mean I trusted her. 'What are you doing here?' I asked suspiciously.

'Charming,' moaned Poppy. She stood up straight and brushed herself down. 'Do you always greet your visitors like that?'

'Not always … just sometimes,' I replied. 'The thing is, not many of my visitors ever arrive at this time of night. So, I'll ask again. What are you doing here?'

'Word spreads quick around Crooked Elbow,' Poppy began. 'Yesterday wasn't the best of days for you, Hugo, so I decided to come and see if you were still in one piece.'

'It's past midnight,' I moaned.

'I was working late,' Poppy explained. 'I've not really got much to go home to if I'm being honest. Listen, I wouldn't have woken you if you were asleep, but I could tell that you weren't. No, you were ready. Ready to attack.' Poppy turned her attention towards the rolling pin. 'You can put that down now,' she said. 'We wouldn't want you to try and whack me again, would we?'

'I guess not,' I shrugged, lowering my arm. At the same time, Poppy put her ear to the shedroom door.

'What's wrong?' I asked.

'Everything,' replied Poppy. 'We need to get you out of here. Now.'

I screwed up my face. 'Why?'

Poppy's throat bobbed as she swallowed nervously. 'You're in grave danger, Hugo,' she revealed. 'And that's the kind of danger that usually results in death!'

21.'IS THIS A TRAP?'

Grave danger or not, I wasn't going anywhere.

Not yet anyway. Not until Poppy Wildheart had explained herself a little more clearly.

'What's going on?' I asked.

Poppy opened her mouth to answer, but then chose, instead, to take the one step needed to reach my shedroom window. 'You can't see much from in here, can you?' she muttered, peeking through the curtains.

'That's never mattered before,' I replied.

'Well, it matters today,' insisted Poppy. 'If we had a better view of Everyday Avenue I could show you what I've seen. It's not safe out there, Hugo. They're right outside your house.'

'Who are?' I asked.

'I don't know,' admitted Poppy. 'They're hard to describe. Whoever they are, though, there's something about them that doesn't quite sit right.'

'Like a three-legged chair?' I said.

'Kind of,' frowned Poppy. 'They're probably waiting for you to leave so they can snatch you.'

'They'll be waiting a long time,' I muttered. 'I was planning on heading back to bed—'

'That's not going to happen,' insisted Poppy, interrupting me mid-sentence. 'Whether you like it or not, I'm not leaving here without you.'

I sat down on my bed before standing up again, unsure of my next move. I didn't know Poppy and I certainly didn't know if I could trust her. Maybe she was one of them. Them being the undesirables who were so keen to get their hands on me. Maybe they were all in it together and this was just a sneaky ploy to get me to go with her. And if that was true – and this really was a trap – then I needed to find out for sure. Thankfully, I knew just the way to do it.

'Is this a trap?' I asked.

'A trap?' Poppy stared at me, confused. 'Why would it be a trap?'

Ah, good question. 'Maybe ... well ... I don't know ... maybe you're not who you seem ... maybe you work for the other side ... the slippery side ... the side of the slimeballs ... or maybe ... maybe ... maybe you just don't like me very much.'

'I barely know you,' replied Poppy.

'That's true,' I shrugged, 'although that hasn't bothered people in the past. Sometimes I think they just look at my face and then come to a snap decision.'

'Your face isn't that bad,' argued Poppy. 'It's actually quite normal from a distance.'

Quite normal from a distance.

And that was when it dropped. The penny, I mean.

Suddenly I knew why Poppy had turned up unexpected in the middle of the night. It was as clear as the spots on my nose. And chin. And forehead. It was so obvious, in fact, that I couldn't quite figure out why I hadn't thought of it before. 'I know why you're here,' I said, wagging a finger at the Big Cheese's personal assistant. 'Although there's got to be a better way to go about things than sneaking up on me in the dark. You could've just asked me when we first met. It would've been easier than all this nonsense.'

'What nonsense?' wondered Poppy.

'*This* nonsense,' I said. 'You know, pretending that I'm in grave danger … demanding that I go with you because it's safer that way …'

'That's all true,' insisted Poppy. 'I'm not just going to make it up—' She stopped suddenly. 'What could I have asked you earlier?'

'You could have asked me out on a date,' I remarked. 'I mean, that is why you're here, isn't it? You want us to go somewhere nice. For dinner most probably. All candles and roses and holding hands under the table. Followed by dancing. Very romantic.'

Poppy pulled a face. 'Is that what you think?'

'I do now,' I said. 'I don't blame you, Poppy. I am quite a catch around Crooked Elbow. Although I do have to warn you, I've not got much money so we might have to settle for a couple of chocolate bars and a jar of pickled eggs. Oh, and I'm not that great a dancer either. I'm very stiff. Like a lamppost in the wind.'

'Lampposts don't move in the wind,' remarked Poppy.

'Exactly,' I said. 'I don't move either. I just stand there, swaying gently from side-to-side—'

'I don't mean to burst your bubble, but this isn't a date,' said Poppy, butting-in. 'I'm old enough to be your mum. Well, your older sister. *Slightly* older sister. You're still at school. You're … you're … you're—' Poppy was stopped mid-sentence by a curious growling sound. 'We've been here too long,' she said, shaking her head. 'We'll talk about this another time. Or maybe we won't. Hopefully not, anyway. For now, though, we need to get out of here.'

'Consider me gone.' Jumping to my feet, I grabbed the suitcase and opened the door to the shedroom. 'After you …'

'Why are you bringing that?' frowned Poppy.

'We've grown very attached,' I replied. 'I don't think of it as a piece of luggage anymore. It's more like a friend.'

Poppy rolled her eyes as she exited the shedroom. 'Which way?' she whispered, looking out over the garden. 'We can't leave via Everyday Avenue because they'll see us … where are you going now?'

'I'm just nipping inside for a moment,' I said, skipping across the grass towards the house. 'I need to change my clothes.'

'Is that really necessary?' grumbled Poppy.

'I can't go out like this,' I remarked. 'Just look at me. I'm practically naked after everything that happened to me yesterday. And I'm missing a shoe.'

Poppy wanted to argue, but knew that she couldn't. 'Be quick,' she said, waving me away. 'I'll be here when you get back.'

'Try not to miss me too much,' I said, winking at her.

'There's no chance of that,' muttered Poppy under her breath.

I stopped at the door and found the key where I had hidden it … in the palm of my hand. No, I don't always keep it there. That would be absurd. Sometimes I let my other hand hold it for a while as well.

One turn later I was inside. The house was both silent and still. Poppy had told me to be quick, but how quick was that? I could hardly rush around in case I crashed into something and woke my parents. The last thing I wanted was Doreen stomping out onto the landing and asking me what I was up to. With that in mind, I tiptoed through the kitchen, along the hallway and up the stairs as quietly as a mouse with three pairs of tiny socks on. I passed Gilbert on the top step and gave him a little wave. He looked pleased to see me … and why wouldn't he? I mean, it wasn't as if he had much else to do. Sitting around all day with a smile on his face and a fishing rod clenched tightly in both hands (but no chance of ever catching any fish) was enough to bore even the most patient of us. Oh, did I forget to say? Gilbert was a garden gnome. My mother had lots of them, more than you could count on the fingers of fifty-three hands, and not all of them were in the garden. Some, like Gilbert, seemed to spend most of their time in the house. In my old bedroom to be precise.

And that was where I was heading next.

I flicked the switch and then gasped out loud as the room lit up. There were gnomes everywhere I looked. All over the

139

floor. Lined up on shelves. Swinging from the lampshade and balancing on the windowsill. Oddly enough, all of them seemed to be turned towards me. For a moment I thought I even saw one blink.

Get a grip, Hugo.

Head down, I crept carefully through my mother's vast collection as I veered towards the wardrobe. If memory served me correctly there were lots of my clothes in there, although it wasn't lots of my clothes that I was interested in. No, it was just one thing in particular.

My tuxedo.

If I was going to be taken seriously as a spy then I would have to start dressing like one. Smart, smooth and sophisticated. If nothing else, it was at least a million times better than my school uniform.

I found the tuxedo squashed at one end of the wardrobe. It had a peculiar smell about it, but nothing compared to the stench that was coming off me already. Shifting some of the gnomes to one side, I created enough floor space so I could get changed. Both the jacket and the trousers were a little on the short side and stopped at my elbows and kneecaps. Still, at least the bow tie looked nice, even if it was tight enough to make me choke.

Dressed and ready to go, I moved swiftly to switch the contents of my pockets from my shorts to my trousers. There was just one last thing I had to do before I left the bedroom, though. Creeping towards the window, I used my nose to make a slight gap in the curtains and peeked outside. As far as I could tell there was nobody out of the ordinary lurking in the shadows. No rogues. No wrong 'uns. No ... wait!

There *was* somebody there.

It was Mr Skinner. Slouched against a tree across the road, he was all but completely hidden except for his dirty white hair that poked out of the bare branches. I looked a little lower and spotted Mr Bones stretched out on the grass by his feet.

Both of them were staring up at my window.

Staring at ... me.

I quickly removed my nose from the curtains and stepped back. Whether they had seen me or not was suddenly the least of my concerns. No, more worrying was the fact that they had found me. My home, just like the Bulging Bellyful, was no longer safe.

Poppy had been right all along. This wasn't a date at all. No, this was much, much worse than that.

This was a disaster.

22.'I HOPE THIS DOESN'T END BADLY …'

I raced out of my old bedroom and turned towards the staircase.

That was when I tripped over Gilbert. When I hit him he was still fishing by the top step. Not now, though. Now he was rolling down the stairs, picking up speed with every bounce.

And he wasn't the only one.

Before I could steady myself, the trip turned to a stumble and I completely lost my balance. Gilbert landed first and smashed into a thousand and three tiny *gnomey* pieces at the foot of the stairs. I followed soon after. I didn't smash, of course, but it still hurt when I flew off the bottom step and crashed into the front door.

I didn't have to wait for long before …

'What was that noise downstairs?' shrieked Doreen.

'Only me, dear,' mumbled Dirk. 'I've got a dodgy stomach …'

'Not that downstairs,' moaned Doreen. 'Downstairs in the house.'

I tried (and failed) to ignore the pain in my arms … hands … wrists … fingers … fingernails … legs … thighs … ankles … no, this could go on forever. Let me start again. I tried to ignore the pain in my body as I pushed myself up and turned towards the kitchen. At the same time, I caught a glimpse of a shadowy figure outside on the doorstep.

Duff … duff … duff …

The pounding knock that followed made my teeth tremble. A moment later the shadowy figure pressed its nose up to the frosted glass in the door. It was Mr Skinner. I could see him clearly, but I doubted he could see me. At least, I hoped not.

Duff … duff … duff …

Mr Skinner knocked again. I knew I had to shift. And I wanted to. More than anything. Walk or run. Shuffle or skip. I just needed to get out of there. And yet I couldn't. Yes, my mind was running wild, but the same couldn't be said for my legs. Quite simply, the tumble I had taken down the stairs had knocked the wind right out of me. I was stuck to the spot. And that spot was beside the door.

There was a *click* and the landing light flickered into life. Next thing I knew my mother had emerged from her bedroom. My father followed soon after. They were both rubbing their eyes. Okay, so it was me who had woken them, but it was Mr Skinner who had forced them out of bed.

My mother was already halfway down the stairs when I heard a voice in my ear.

'Hide!'

The next thing I knew I was being dragged across the

hallway by my ankles. To my surprise, it was Poppy who was doing the dragging. Stronger than she looked, she only stopped when we were both concealed by the coat stand that was opposite the door. Without thinking, I reached up and grabbed my father's smelly old overcoat that he used for gardening and threw it over the pair of us.

Duff … duff … duff …

'I'm coming, I'm coming.' That was Doreen. She had finished rubbing her eyes and had now settled into a steady stream of grumbling as she reached the foot of the stairs. As far as I could tell she hadn't spotted us. Not yet. But she would do. I was sure of it. 'Do you know what time it is?' she snapped. 'Who would possibly come calling at such an unacceptable hour?'

The huge shadow of Mr Skinner vanished from the glass. At the same time, the letterbox flipped open.

'My humblest apologies, madam,' he said creepily. 'I do not wish to cause you any distress.'

'Well, you might not wish it …' muttered Doreen.

'Then I apologise again,' insisted Skinner. 'Wholeheartedly. In fact, if you open the door I can show you just how apologetic I really am.'

Doreen looked over her shoulder at Dirk, who simply shrugged as he joined her at the door. 'We should probably find out what he wants,' he suggested. 'It could be important.'

'You would say that,' sighed Doreen. With that, she turned the key. 'I hope this doesn't end badly …'

'Good evening … or should that be good morning,' said

Skinner, as the door slowly opened. Without being invited in, he took a clumsy step over the threshold. It was a smart move. Not only did he now fill the entire doorway, but his presence also made it impossible for the door to be closed on him.

'Good nothing,' scowled Doreen. 'I'm not overly fond of visitors at the best of times … and this is anything but the best of times! I'm tired. I need my beauty sleep.'

'Yes, I can see that,' nodded Skinner in agreement. 'I promise I will keep you no longer than is necessary. My name is Mr Skinner and I come here on a matter of great urgency.'

'Who's your friend?' asked Dirk, peeking under my mother's arm.

'My friend?' Skinner hesitated a moment before yanking on Mr Bones's lead. 'We are not friends,' he said coldly. 'We are simply associates.'

'Well your associate is simply on all fours,' remarked Dirk. 'And he's wearing a collar. That's a little peculiar, don't you think? What is he? Half-man, half-dog? Or half-dog, half-man?'

'Or just a horrible stinking beast?' added Doreen.

Springing to his feet, Mr Bones lunged at my mother before the lead tightened around his neck.

'Ha! Very good,' laughed Skinner, wagging a finger in Doreen's face. 'I guess it takes one to know one.'

'Does he bite?' asked Dirk, edging away from the door.

'Only if you let him,' revealed Skinner. 'Now, I've not woken you up to talk about my associate. In fact, I've not come to see you at all. Neither of you. I'm here for the boy.'

'What boy?' frowned Doreen.

'The boy who lives here,' pressed Skinner. 'His name is Hugo Dare. Also known as the Pink Weasel.'

'Just Pink Weasel,' said Dirk proudly. 'There is no *the*.'

Doreen glared at my father. 'There is no boy living here,' she said, turning back towards the door.

'Except the Pink Weasel,' grinned Skinner.

'I don't know anybody called Pink Weasel – the or not – and there is no boy living here in this house,' repeated Doreen, stone-faced and serious.

'No, but Hugo is in his shedroom,' announced Dirk. Without warning, my mother stepped back and stamped on his slippered foot. 'Ouch!' he cried. 'What did you do that for?'

'Sorry,' muttered Doreen. 'I meant to put it in your mouth—'

'Enough,' snarled Skinner, pressing a finger to my mother's lips. 'There is a boy. I know, you know, even Mr Bones knows. Now fetch him for me.'

'That's not going to happen,' said Doreen fiercely.

'You should listen to her,' said Dirk, nodding repeatedly. 'She always gets her own way.'

'Not this time.' Mr Skinner leant forward until he was eyeball-to-eyeball with my mother. 'I shall make this very easy for you,' he began. 'Bring me the boy ... otherwise you'll find out why I need to keep Mr Bones on a lead!'

My mother froze, whilst my father simply shivered.

'We have to do something,' I whispered to Poppy.

146

'I know,' she replied.

'Any ideas?' I asked.

'Just one.' Poppy took a breath as she grabbed hold of the coat stand. 'Get ready, Hugo, because things are about to get really, really messy …'

23.'I DID TRY TO WARN YOU.'

Doreen tried to close the door, surprised to find that Mr Skinner's foot was preventing her from doing so.

'That should've hurt ... but it didn't,' Skinner remarked. With that, he rolled up his trouser. 'It's a metal leg,' he revealed. 'Pain-free and impossible to damage.'

A determined Doreen slammed the door again just to be certain.

'Making me mad is not your best course of action,' said Skinner, refusing to budge.

'I don't care,' remarked Doreen. 'You don't scare me.'

'No ... *um* ... me neither,' said Dirk unconvincingly.

'In that case ...' Mr Skinner reached down and began to loosen the leash around Mr Bones's throat. 'I did try to warn you.'

With the human hound about to be let loose, Poppy jumped to her feet and raced across the hallway with the coat stand out in front of her like a jouster's lance. She spun it around in her hands until it was pointing the right way.

The right way being straight at the door.

'Move!' yelled Poppy.

My mother did just that and crashed into my father, the force enough to send the two of them stumbling back into the hallway. Mr Skinner and Mr Bones, however, weren't so quick to react. Before they knew it, Poppy had crashed into them at speed. Skinner took the brunt of the blow, the coat stand striking him firmly in the chest. I watched in amazement as he staggered backwards off the doorstep and rolled over in the front garden. Whether he meant it or not, he didn't let go of the lead and Mr Bones went with him. As a final flourish, Poppy threw the coat stand at the two bewildered goons before slamming the door shut.

'You need to get out of here, Hugo,' she said, gasping for breath.

'I don't know who this woman is, but that seems like a good idea,' agreed Doreen.

'Go out the back way,' said Dirk, pointing towards the garden. 'Over the fence. We'll cover you. I might even fetch some of that exploding toothpaste and stick it right up their—'

My father was interrupted by the sound of a furious Mr Skinner pounding on the door.

'Go!' cried Poppy.

I turned away and hurried towards the kitchen. I didn't want to leave either my parents or Poppy, but what choice did I have? Mr Skinner and Mr Bones weren't after them; they were after me. Fact. Deal with it. I know I have.

Outside, I found the suitcase just where I had left it. I grabbed it with one hand and tossed it over the fence at the bottom of the garden without breaking stride. If anything, it would provide a soft landing for me.

Here goes nothing …

Without missing a beat, I threw myself at the fence and then clung on the best I could. Bad move. Who knew it would give way immediately and topple over like a huge, wooden domino? Not me, that was for sure. But that was exactly what happened. Before I knew it I was laid flat out on the pavement with the fence beneath me. I looked both left then right, relieved to find that there was no passing traffic or nosey pedestrians to witness my misfortune. I had barely shifted when I heard voices coming from Everyday Avenue. They were followed by a shout, a scream and, unless I was mistaken, a squawk. Flattened fence or not, feeling sorry for myself was no longer an option. Like Poppy had said, I had to get out of there.

Scrambling to my feet, I snatched the suitcase from out of the gutter it had landed in and set off at speed along the pavement.

But not for long.

I slowed my step at the sight of a vehicle parked up on the opposite side of the road. It was a bright yellow pick-up truck. The same bright yellow pick-up truck that had picked me up outside Smog Suites the previous day.

The same bright yellow pick-up truck that belonged to Frankie Fingertips and Candy Gloss.

I could've turned and run, but then why would I? The pick-up was empty with both its engine and lights switched off. Frankie and Candy were nowhere to be seen. As far as I could tell …

And that was the problem; I was only fifty per-cent certain. Maybe fifty-one. And a half. I had a decision to make … and I decided to keep on walking forward.

For some reason, I chose to count my footsteps as I edged closer to the pick-up.

Four … eight … twelve …

I kept my pace steady and my head completely still. The next few seconds were vital.

Sixteen … twenty … twenty-three … no, that's not right. Twenty-four …

I held my breath as I drew level with the truck. Without making it too obvious, I glanced out the corner of my eye. I was right; the pick-up was empty. There was nobody inside.

Twenty-eight … thirty-two … thirty-six …

I took a breath for the first time in ages when I finally reached forty footsteps. I had done it. I had left the pick-up behind me.

A moment later and the gentle purr of an engine suggested otherwise.

I knew without looking that the pick-up was on the move. Right on cue, the purr grew louder and a yellow bonnet rolled into view. It didn't take a genius to guess what would happen next. Frankie had snatched me before and he would surely try again.

That didn't mean, however, that he would succeed.

'Greetings, kid.' I turned to see Frankie hanging out of the window. 'I adore this time of day,' he said, glancing up at the night sky. 'When it's deathly dark and as dark as death. Everybody normal is fast asleep in their beds, which means us *not so* normal folk can do what the heck we like. And doing what I like is what I love the most. Hey, where did I leave my manners? Do you want a lift? There's nothing to be afraid of.'

'Who said I was afraid?' I replied.

'Not me,' laughed Frankie. 'Listen, kid, I know we've had our ups and downs these past few days, but that's no reason to hold it against me. I'm perfectly harmless.'

'I'm harmless, too,' shrieked a voice from the driver's seat. 'Tell him, Pudding Bowl. Tell him what a good girl I am.'

The truck scuffed against the kerb as Candy joined her partner in poking her head through the window.

'Hiya,' she giggled. 'Now, what's a little pumpkin seed like you doing wandering these mean old streets at night? Hop in and we'll take you home before something unpleasant happens to you.'

'I think it already has,' I muttered to myself.

'There you go again,' said Frankie, shaking his trilby at me. 'Always thinking bad of us.'

'I don't think he understands,' sighed Candy.

'No, I don't think he does,' agreed Frankie. 'He doesn't seem to realise that we're here to take care of him. To protect him from the others. The others that aren't quite as friendly as we are.' Quick as a flash, Frankie reached out and grabbed me by the wrist. 'You do know that I can drag you into this car, don't you, kid?' he growled. 'I've done it before … I can do it again.'

I tried to pull myself free, but his grip held firm.

Without slowing, I turned away from Frankie and looked along the road ahead. There was a crossroads fast approaching. It was where three roads met. Under normal circumstances I would have been forced to come to a halt. And so, too, would the pick-up. But these weren't normal circumstances.

And that was why I started to run.

'There's no point trying to escape,' scowled Frankie, as the pick-up increased its speed.

'Let go!' I cried, struggling to shake him off. 'Just … let … go!'

'Can't do that, kid,' insisted Frankie.

'You might have to.' Not only was Candy's head back inside the pick-up, but her nose was now pressed up to the windscreen. 'There are two cars heading our way,' she squealed, pointing wildly at the crossroads. 'One from the left and one from the other. Unless you want us to get walloped from both sides then I'm going to have to hit the brakes.'

'I hear you, Sugar Stick,' nodded Frankie. 'But the same applies to you, kid,' he remarked, turning back to me. 'You'd better stop, too. Running straight into the traffic is a risk that nobody would want to take.'

I ignored him and kept on moving.

True to her word, Candy stamped down on the brakes and the pick-up began to shudder. It was enough to make Frankie let go of my arm.

All of a sudden I was free. But it was too late for me to stop. Instead, I staggered forward into the road. The last thing I did was lift the suitcase in front of my face, ready for the moment.

That's the moment I became the human filling in the middle of a car sandwich.

24. 'YOU'RE LOOKING THE WRONG WAY!'

I didn't.

Get hit, I mean. I should've done. Definitely. But somehow I never did.

Stood stranded in the road, I was shocked to find that both cars had skidded to a halt only inches from my feet. At first I thought it was a stroke of luck of massive proportions. And then I decided it was something else entirely.

Something slightly more deliberate.

I lowered the suitcase and looked over at the nearest car to me. It was a sleek black limousine. Not the usual kind of vehicle you'd find cruising the streets of Crooked Elbow after dark. I was still gazing at it when the passenger door opened and out stepped Wheezing Wally. It was the middle of the night but he was still wearing sunglasses. At a guess, Sneezing Stan must've been sat in the driver's seat.

Wally closed the door and began to march towards me.

'You're looking the wrong way!'

Spinning on my heels, I turned to see that the voice was

coming from the other car that had braked beside me. It was a white Mini. And sat inside, with one hand on the steering wheel and the other hanging out the window, beckoning me to join her, was Poppy.

'Stop staring and start moving!' she yelled. 'Get in!'

I didn't need telling twice.

Sliding smoothly over the bonnet of the Mini, I yanked open the door and threw the suitcase onto the back seat. I followed it a moment later, just in time to see the limousine roll forward. It was heading straight for us.

But then so, too, was the pick-up.

Back on the move, Candy was driving blind into the middle of the road. I knew what was going to happen next, even if nobody else did. Sure enough, there was a horrible *crunching* sound as the pick-up and the limousine crashed into one another. And that was all I got to see as the Mini surged into life. Spinning the steering wheel, Poppy performed a smart U-turn before speeding off the way she had just come. I gave a little wave as we disappeared into the distance.

So long, suckers.

'Seatbelt,' said Poppy, without looking at me.

I did as she asked and strapped myself in. 'That was close,' I panted. 'How did you know where I'd be?'

'I didn't,' Poppy admitted. 'I just got lucky'.

'Lucky … for me,' I grinned. I had a sudden thought that immediately wiped the smile from my face. 'What did Mr Skinner and Mr Bones do to my parents?'

'Nothing,' revealed Poppy to my relief. 'Not once they

realised you were no longer there. In the end your mother chased them off, whilst your father tried to throw toothpaste at them. I didn't really understand that, but it seemed to do the trick. After that, I told them who I was and that I'd come and find you.'

'And you have,' I said. 'I think I owe you an apology. I didn't trust you at first, but I was wrong. You're not a bit like the Big Cheese's other personal assistants.'

'Pleased to hear it.' Poppy shifted awkwardly in her seat so she could glance over her shoulder. 'I don't think they're following us. We've done it. We've escaped.'

I held my breath and waited for something to go drastically wrong. It usually did when somebody made a comment like that. I was still waiting, though, when the Mini swung around two corners in quick succession. 'This isn't the way to the SICK Bucket,' I remarked.

'That's because we're not going there,' said Poppy, proving me correct. I fell back in my seat as the Mini shot forward. 'There is somewhere, though,' she revealed. 'Somewhere I'd rather not go if I'm being honest, but needs must …'

'Is it safe?' I asked, crossing my fingers.

'Let's hope so,' muttered Poppy, as we sped off towards our mystery location, 'because this is the last place on earth that anyone would ever dream of looking for you.'

25.'WOULD YOU LIKE A GUIDED TOUR?'

Exactly seven minutes later we drove through a pair of wrought iron gates.

The gates opened onto a long, twisted gravel driveway that was illuminated by spotlights and flanked on either side by a combination of hedges and shrubs, all of which were immaculately cut back and cared for. Beyond the driveway there was a beautifully landscaped garden that stretched as far as the eye could see and then a little bit more after that. And let's not forget about the fountain. With its six-tiered stone centrepiece accompanied by four flamingos, it was as spectacular a fountain as I'd ever seen (note to reader – I haven't see many others. If any.) They weren't real flamingos, of course. I mean, I don't think so. Maybe they were. Nevertheless, real or fake, both the fountain and its surrounding garden made for an incredibly impressive sight.

Perhaps more impressive, however, was the house at the end of the driveway.

Wait. Did I say house? My mistake. I meant to say

mansion. Because this house was huge. Like thirteen normal houses stuck together and then piled on top of one another. I studied it a little more closely, but all I could see were windows, more windows and even more windows after that. I could go on, but I don't think I'm able. Not until I scrape my jaw up off the floor at least.

I had already decided to snap out of my trance and stop staring in wonder when, without warning, Poppy stamped on the brakes and my entire body lurched forward. When I looked again the Mini had skidded to a halt right outside the front entrance, an impenetrable-looking wooden door.

'This isn't quite what I was expecting,' I said, climbing out of the car. 'Who lives here?'

'Nobody,' revealed Poppy, as she joined me outside. 'Not at the moment, anyway. It's currently empty.'

'Oh, I get it,' I said, wagging a finger at her. 'We're going to let ourselves in, aren't we? They call that breaking and entering—'

'We're not going to burgle the place if that's what you mean,' remarked Poppy. 'Besides, I know a much easier way to get inside …'

To my surprise, she removed a key from her pocket and slotted it into the keyhole. One *click* later and she lowered the handle and forced the door to one side.

'Don't just stand there with your tongue hanging out,' moaned Poppy, stepping over the threshold. 'Come on in so I can close the door. We can lie low in here until first light. We'll be safe … fingers crossed.'

I was all set to do as she asked when I spotted a wooden

plaque stuck on the wall beside me.

'Wildheart Hall,' I read out loud. I repeated it several times until it seemed to stick in my brain. 'But Wildheart is your name,' I said, confused.

'Well spotted,' sighed Poppy. 'Thanks for reminding me.'

'Wow!' I gasped. 'Don't tell me this is your parents' house?'

'Then I won't.' Poppy ushered me inside before quickly closing the door behind us, locking it instantly. 'It did belong to my parents once, though. Just not anymore.'

'Bit too big for them, was it?' I wondered. 'Is that why they moved out?'

'Something like that.' Shuffling away from the door, Poppy flicked a switch on the wall that illuminated the entrance. 'They ... erm ... did more than just move out,' she mumbled. 'They died.'

Whoops.

At that very moment I should have been gazing in awe at the sheer splendour that surrounded me. Instead, I was shrinking into my tight-fitting tuxedo. As usual I had said the wrong thing at exactly the wrong time. I had put my foot in it without even lifting my leg. Now I just hoped I could pull it out without Poppy noticing.

'Sorry,' I said quickly. 'Sometimes I just speak without thinking ... I'm doing it now ... I could say anything ... I can't control myself ... reindeer ... cabbage soup ... trampoline—'

'Stop that,' butted-in Poppy. 'And there's no need to

apologise either. My parents died a long time ago. I was young when it happened. But I did live here for a while before that, even if I can't really remember much about it. These days, however, I tend to avoid the place.'

I screwed up my face. Maybe it was time to shift the conversation in a different direction. 'Do you think the new owner will mind us being here?' I asked.

'No, I'm pretty sure *I* don't mind us being here.' Poppy pulled a face of her own as she held out her arms. 'This is mine,' she said with a shrug. 'All of it. Wildheart Hall belongs to me.'

'You?' I pointed at Poppy in disbelief. 'This is … yours?'

'Unfortunately so,' sighed Poppy. The ceiling was so high and the entrance was so vast that her voice seemed to echo forever. 'Would you like a guided tour?'

I nodded. Why not? Twenty-three minutes later, however, and I had started to regret it. Not only was every room identical – both large and luxurious – but we had only made it halfway around the house. I was exhausted and I'm not ashamed to admit it. Poppy, thankfully, seemed to realise this and cut the tour short. Heading downstairs into the basement, she led me, instead, into a tiny kitchen.

'This is where the staff would eat,' revealed Poppy, as, one by one, she opened up the cupboards and drawers. 'I used to like it down here as a child. It was always warm and there was lots of laughter. Are you hungry?'

'Starving,' I replied, sitting down at a long wooden table.

'I was hoping you wouldn't say that,' said Poppy. 'There's not really much food in. Nothing fresh anyway.

Although … if I remember correctly … we always used to keep a packet or two of …' Poppy reached up on tip-toes and removed something from the back of one of the cupboards. 'Ah, chocolate biscuits,' she said, placing them down on the table. 'They could have been here for years for all I know. And … what's that?' she said, reaching up again. 'Fish paste. Mmm … that could be even older.'

'Let me worry about that,' I said, licking my lips. By the time Poppy had joined me at the table I was already working my way through what she had discovered. I actually used my finger to spread the paste on the biscuit. It was an unusual combination, but not the worst I'd ever tasted.

'Enjoying yourself?' asked Poppy, grabbing a biscuit before I could finish them all off.

'Very much so.' My mouth was full, but that didn't stop me from talking. 'I like Wildheart Hall,' I said, nodding to myself. 'It's probably about thirty-seven rooms too big, and colder than a penguin's pencil case, but it's still pretty cool. And it's yours. That's bonkers. It must be worth a fortune.' I stopped for a moment as a strange thought hit me for the very first time. 'Why do you bother working for SICK?' I blurted out. 'You could just sell the house and live off the money for the rest of your life.'

'You're right,' agreed Poppy. 'I could. But then why would I want to? That'd just be boring. And working for SICK is anything but boring.' A loud burp from yours truly was enough to stop her mid-flow. 'Talking of sick, have you finished yet?' Poppy asked. 'You've eaten quite a lot. Probably too much. Especially in such a short space of time.'

'Yes, I've finished,' I nodded. 'And I liked it. I liked it a lot. Although I'm not sure my belly would agree with me.'

'There's one more room I want to show you,' said Poppy, rising up from the table. 'Come on. It'll take your mind off your stomach.'

We slowly made our way out of the basement. Aside from our footsteps, it seemed eerily quiet in Wildheart Hall. And eerily quiet meant seriously spooky. I was starting to understand why Poppy didn't live here. Not on her own at least. Maybe things would be different if she could find another three hundred people to share it with her.

'The Great Room,' announced Poppy, as we came to a halt. As its name suggested, the room was gigantic. From top to bottom, it was crammed full of all manner of furniture from cabinets and couches, to chandeliers and chaise-longues. Not only that, but there was an antique fireplace and sparkling suit of armour at one end of the room, and a huge grandfather clock and ornate mirror at the other.

'We can sleep in here,' said Poppy. At the same time, she locked the door, trapping us inside. 'Well, one of us can. The other will have to stay awake and keep watch. We'll take turns.'

'I'll go first,' I said.

Poppy tried not to smile. 'Are you sure, Hugo? You don't really seem like a first watch kind of spy. At a guess you're probably more of a fall asleep three seconds later kind of spy.'

'Bit rude,' I frowned. 'I never fall asleep on the job … oh, excuse me.' I stopped for a moment so I could yawn. 'I always do that when I'm not tired,' I said awkwardly.

'Yes, I believe you,' laughed Poppy. 'Okay, have it your way. I'll sleep first and get a few hours rest. We'll switch the lights off and leave the curtains open so you can keep checking outside. Wake me up if you see anything.'

'Anything?' I said.

'Anything out of the ordinary,' explained Poppy. Settling down in the nearest armchair to her, she snatched a blanket up off the floor and covered herself from head-to-toe. 'And that includes *anybody* out of the ordinary. Those same anybody's that have been chasing you these past few days.'

I waited until Poppy had closed her eyes before I strolled across the Great Room and turned out the lights. I was immediately plunged into darkness. I let my eyes adjust and then wandered over to the window. The grounds of Wildheart Hall were lit up by a number of spotlights, perfect for me to see the entire driveway and beyond. Thankfully, everything seemed perfectly normal. Quite peaceful really. Albeit a little bit creepy.

With nothing to do, I began to pace slowly up and down the Great Room in a bid to calm my nerves. As luck would have it, there was an enormous rug beneath my feet that filled much of the floor space and, therefore, softened my footsteps. I stopped when I reached the fireplace and turned around. I was safe and there was no reason why that would change anytime soon. Nobody would ever find me here. How could they?

Before I knew it I was back where I had started. At the window. I looked outside for a second time, but nothing had changed. All clear.

My eyelids felt heavy. I guessed at the time – somewhere between two and three in the morning – and then tried to figure out how long Poppy had been asleep for. That was probably between two and three as well. Two and three minutes. I had a long wait.

I continued to pace up and down. Now I had another problem, though. The toilet was calling and I was eager to pay it a visit. I had spotted several bathrooms on Poppy's guided tour, but I couldn't recall where they were or how to find them, especially in the dark. Without stopping, I peered around the Great Room for anything that could come to my aid. There was a coal scuttle by the fireplace that would probably do the trick. Okay, a bucket would've been better, but desperate times call for desperate measures. And I was desperate. Desperately so, in fact.

I reached the window for the umpteenth time, crossed my legs and did everything I could not to groan out loud. This was getting painful now. Still, it would all be over soon. All I had to do was make my way up the other end and grab the coal scuttle and I could get down to business. I was about to turn when I remembered to look outside.

Pressing my nose up to the glass, I blinked several times and gazed out across the driveway.

And that was when I saw them …

26.'YOU HAVE SEVEN MINUTES.'

Them.

Mr Skinner and Mr Bones.

Frankie Fingertips and Candy Gloss.

Wheezing Wally and Sneezing Stan.

Captain Olga Kartoffel.

And, last but not least, Mickey the Fix. He was laughing to himself, but that was nothing new. He was always laughing to himself.

Spinning away from the window, I kept my head down as I scurried across the Great Room. 'Wake up!' I said, trying not to raise my voice in case they could hear me outside.

'I am awake,' mumbled Poppy, even though she clearly wasn't. Sitting up in the armchair, she began to rub her eyes. 'What is it?'

'They're here,' I said, pointing behind me.

Poppy took a moment to yawn. 'Who are?'

'*They* are,' I blurted out. 'Every last one of them. They've found us.'

I left Poppy where she was and hurried back to the window. The goons had stopped about a stone's throw away from the house. Stood in a line, they seemed to be contemplating their next move. That was to our advantage. For all they knew, there could have been hundreds of us in the house. All fully-armed and ready to go. There wasn't, of course. There was just the two of us.

'This is bad,' I muttered under my breath.

'Very,' agreed Poppy, creeping up behind me. 'How did they know where to find us? This house is a secret and I'm sure we weren't followed. And even if we were, why has it taken them so long to show themselves?' Poppy ducked down beneath the window. 'Empty your pockets,' she said suddenly.

'My pockets?' I repeated.

Poppy nodded frantically. 'Something doesn't feel right ... and your pockets might hold the key!'

'There are definitely no keys in there,' I said, 'but there is all of this ...'

I knelt down beside her and laid the contents out on the rug. There was snotty tissues and scraps of paper. Half a pack of chewing gum, a shark's tooth and a rubber duck. You know, just normal stuff you pick up along on the way. Oh, and let's not forget about that tube my father had given me.

Now it was Poppy's turn to look confused. 'Toothpaste?'

'*Exploding* toothpaste,' I said, correcting her. 'Not really for brushing your teeth with.'

'That might come in useful,' nodded Poppy, handing it back to me. 'The rest of this is just rubbish, though. And you've nothing else, have you? Nothing unusual. Unless ...'

I followed her gaze across the Great Room. She was

staring at the suitcase. 'But that's not even mine,' I insisted.

'Exactly.' Poppy rushed over and snatched it up off the floor. 'Fetch me something … something sharp … that knife should do the trick.'

The knife in question was actually a letter opener on display above the fireplace. I passed it to Poppy who, without hesitation, used it to cut a hole in the lining of the suitcase.

'Whoa! Be careful,' I cried out. 'I've grown quite attached to that grubby old thing.'

'And it's grown quite attached to you,' muttered Poppy, as she slashed at the fabric. 'So much so, in fact, that I think it might be the cause of all your problems … yes, I'm right … take a look at this.'

Carefully, as if she was handling something precious, Poppy removed a small black box from inside the lining. There were a number of dials at one end and a flashing light at the other.

'What is it?' I asked.

'A tracker,' explained Poppy. 'I've used them lots of times before but I've never seen one hidden in a suitcase. Still, needs must when you need to track someone.'

I stared at her blankly before it all fell into place. 'I'm the someone, aren't I? They've been tracking me. And this suitcase is the reason I've been so easy to find!'

'You could be right,' nodded Poppy. 'But that would only work if you've been dragging around the suitcase ever since Brooke Keeper first gave it to you—' Poppy stopped suddenly. 'Tell me you haven't, have you?'

'Well, it's funny you should say that,' I mumbled. 'It's funny because the suitcase has never left my side. Don't look at me like that, Pops. I've tried to throw it away on numerous occasions but it keeps on coming back to me.'

Poppy turned the dials on the box until the light went out. 'There,' she said, showing me the tracker before she stuck it in her pocket. 'I've turned it off now. They can't track you anymore.'

'They don't need to,' I moaned. 'They've already found me.'

I lifted my head and looked out of the window, just in time to see Mr Skinner step forward and break the line.

'We know you're in there, Maggot,' he called out. 'There's no point hiding and there's even less point trying to run away. You are surrounded.'

I watched as Wheezing Wally and Sneezing Stan moved across the grass towards the right of the house, whilst Captain Kartoffel and Mickey the Fix turned left. They were trying to block every exit. Trapping us inside.

'As unexpected as it seems, we have buried our differences and joined together,' Skinner announced. 'We even have a name. The Undesirable Eight. That was my idea. It has a nice ring to it, don't you think?' Mr Skinner hesitated, almost as if he expected me to agree with him. 'For tonight, at least, we hunt as one,' he said eventually. 'That way we can all be winners!'

'We'll see about that,' muttered Poppy to herself.

Mr Skinner took another *clunky* stride towards Wildheart Hall. 'There are many ways we can do this,' he began, 'but I do not believe in making things difficult. Not for you … not for me … not for any of us. That is why I am prepared to give you seven minutes. Seven minutes to leave the house and come quietly.'

'Seven minutes?' I snorted. 'Why not ten? Or even five? Yes, five makes more sense. Maybe Skinner hasn't thought of that. I should probably tell him—'

Poppy put a hand on my shoulder and pushed me back down before I stood up and did something we both regretted.

'If you do not leave in seven minutes, however, we will have to come and drag you out ourselves,' continued Skinner. 'That is not to be advised. It will almost certainly end badly. Right, the countdown has begun. You have seven minutes … that is four hundred and twenty seconds … four hundred and nineteen … four hundred and eighteen …'

'I should probably do as he asks,' I said, ducking under the window ledge. 'I don't want to put you in any danger. It's the safest thing to do.'

'It's the daftest thing to do,' argued Poppy.

'There are eight of them, though,' I remarked. 'And they're all undesirable. There's no way we can escape from that many.'

'Isn't there?' Poppy kept out of sight as she began to crawl away from the window. 'There's a secret tunnel that runs from here, in the Great Room, all the way to an old barn deep in the grounds of Wildheart Hall,' she revealed. 'We can get out that way and nobody will ever know.'

'Really?' My heart began to leap like a salmon with a

skyrocket strapped to its scales. 'That's amazing … the perfect plan … completely fool proof … absolutely—'

'Slow down.' Poppy's head seemed to turn three hundred and sixty degrees as she studied our surroundings. 'Yes, there's a tunnel … I just don't know where it is!'

27.'ANY LUCK?'

I was about to speak when Mr Skinner beat me to it.

'Three hundred seconds and counting,' he bellowed.

'What's that?' I said, my brain ticking over. 'Six minutes?'

'Five,' said Poppy, correcting me.

'Wow! That last minute just flew by,' I grumbled. 'It never goes that quick when I'm at school.'

'Not funny, Hugo,' scowled Poppy.

'I was trying to lighten the mood before we search for this tunnel,' I insisted.

'*Secret* tunnel,' remarked Poppy, correcting me again. 'And there's a good reason it's been kept secret all this time. Look ...' Poppy gestured wildly around the Great Room. 'It's so big in here we could be searching for weeks and still not find anything.'

'Don't give up now, Pops,' I said, patting her firmly on the back. 'I'll start one side and you start the other. We can do this. We're SICK.'

Poppy drew a breath. 'You're right,' she said, hurrying over to the nearest wall. 'We can do anything if we put our minds to it.'

I waited until she wasn't looking before I screwed up my face. At least somebody believed in us. Because I certainly didn't.

'Two hundred and fifty …' shouted Mr Skinner.

I began to work my way around the room, weaving in and out of every nook and cranny in search of … what exactly? It would've helped if I knew what I was looking for. Some kind of handle perhaps. Or a knob. Or a button. Or a lever. Or a switch. Or a …

'Two hundred …'

I pressed on regardless and checked under armchairs, lifted up lamps and scoured under side tables, but there was nothing there of any note.

The secret tunnel (if such a thing even existed) had no wish to come out of hiding.

'One hundred and fifty …'

'Any luck?' I called out.

'Not in the slightest,' replied Poppy irritably. 'Have you tried looking on the floor yet?'

'There's a rug on the floor,' I replied.

'Well spotted,' muttered Poppy. 'Look under the rug.'

I glanced down at my feet and frowned. 'The rug's really big.'

'And you're a big boy,' moaned Poppy, 'so get down there and have a look.'

'One hundred …'

I reluctantly did as she asked. First things first, I tried to peel the rug up off the floorboards, but failed tragically. Not only was it incredibly heavy, but it seemed to have stuck itself down over time. Impossible to just roll up and shift to one side like Poppy seemed to imagine. No, the only way to find out for sure if it was concealing the entrance to the secret tunnel was to get up close and personal. Wish me luck.

Starting at one corner, I lifted the rug just enough for me to prop it up with my head before I crawled underneath. From there on in, all I could do was lay flat on my stomach and slither along with my arms out-stretched. Occasionally, I had to take a detour around a piece of furniture, but it wasn't enough to stop me. If the secret tunnel was anywhere on the floor then I was sure to find it.

That was a very big *if*, though.

'Fifty seconds …'

I popped my head out of the rug and gasped for breath. I could see Poppy in front of me, shuffling sideways like a confused crab as her hands moved swiftly over the surface of the wall in search of anything that would open the tunnel. I moved swiftly too, and ducked back under the rug. This time, however, I chose a different route than before. This time I turned and twisted, swerved and spiralled, but it was all to no avail. I was becoming increasingly desperate. Time was running out. Any second …

'Your seven minutes are up,' announced Mr Skinner, 'and I still don't see you. That's a bad move, Maggot. I warned you what would happen if you failed to do as I asked. Now you must face the consequences.'

I collapsed face-first onto the floor and forgot about the rug as it dropped down on top of me. Ouch. That hurt more than I expected. Still, that was nothing compared to the pain

I would feel when the Undesirable Eight finally got their hands on me. Especially if it was Mr Bones and his grubby paws.

'Hugo.' That was Poppy. 'Where are you?'

'Here,' I replied, my voice dampened by the weight on top of me.

'Where's here?' she asked. 'I can't see you … unless … you're not that huge lump in the middle of the rug, are you?'

'Yes, that's me.' I sneezed as a huge pile of dust shot up one nostril and got stuck in my throat. 'What's wrong?' I asked.

'Nothing,' cried Poppy. 'The exact opposite, in fact. Something's right. I've found it. The secret tunnel.'

I scrambled towards the edge of the rug and crawled out. It took me a moment to get my bearings before I spotted Poppy stood beside the fireplace.

'I touched the tip,' she said, gesturing towards a sharp-looking sword that was attached to the suit of armour. 'And then this happened.'

This was a door. A door that had appeared after a panel of the wall had mysteriously opened.

Grinning from ear to ear, I leapt to my feet and set off for the other end of the Great Room. I had barely moved, though, before the alarming sound of stomping feet and raised voices stopped me dead in my tracks.

The Undesirable Eight had got inside Wildheart Hall.

I took one look at Poppy and nodded. She nodded back. We had come to an agreement. Whether I liked it or not, I was too far away from the tunnel to make it there in time.

Touching the tip of the sword, Poppy hurried through the opening before the door closed behind her. She had vanished from view. As had the secret tunnel.

I, however, hadn't.

Stood in the middle of the Great Room, I was just about to make my move when I heard a series of unwelcome noises.

First it was footsteps.

Then it was the squeaky creak of the door handle.

Then it was a ferocious *thud ... thud ... thud.*

And that was the ferocious thud of somebody hammering on the door, desperate to come in.

28.'ONLY ME.'

The door to the Great Room began to shudder.

Poppy had locked us in, but that wouldn't keep them out forever.

Thud … thud … thud …

No, scratch that. By the sound of things that wouldn't keep them out at all. Which meant that, at a guess, I probably had no more than a second or less to find a hiding place. My eyes returned to the rug, but didn't linger there for long. All that dust would only make me sneeze again and, besides, it wouldn't be hard to spot a large Hugo Dare-shaped lump in the middle of the floor.

Instead, I opted for the fireplace. There was a fire guard blocking the way, which I gently eased to one side so I could slip in behind it. It was a tight squeeze, but I'd known tighter. Careful not to make a sound, I moved the guard back into place and then waited for whoever entered.

One … two … two-and-a-half … *crash!*

I tried not to jump as the door to the Great Room was knocked clean off its hinges. It hardly came as a surprise to see Frankie Fingertips and Candy Gloss had taken its place in the empty opening. They had a history of knocking down doors, after all.

'Only me,' announced Frankie, poking his head into the room.

'And me,' said Candy, skipping past him.

'Be careful, Treacle Toes,' Frankie warned, as he wandered in behind her. 'The kid's dangerous. He might leap out at you at any moment.'

'The kid would actually have to be in here to leap out at me,' remarked Candy, spinning around in circles. 'And here he most certainly ain't. Anyone can see that.'

'Maybe, Baby,' agreed Frankie, 'but that doesn't mean we have to tell the rest of those jerks that.' He grabbed Candy by the hand and pulled her towards him. 'We don't have to tell them anything,' he whispered in her ear. 'I don't know about you, Pineapple Chunks, but I ain't planning on sharing the prize with no one. Those fools don't deserve it.'

'I like the sound of that,' purred Candy. 'If … *when* we find the kid, we'll keep him to ourselves. It can be our little secret.'

'What can be our little secret?'

Frankie and Candy turned towards the exit. I did too and spotted a grinning Mickey the Fix leant nonchalantly against the door frame.

'Mickey hopes you're not making plans without him,' chuckled the handyman.

'As if we would,' said Frankie, feigning innocence. 'Why would you say such a thing?'

'Mickey heard you talking,' the handyman revealed.

'With ears like this you don't tend to miss much.'

'That may be so,' began Frankie, 'but those ears of yours are actually mistaken. There are no secrets in here. Just me and my precious girl looking for the kid.'

'Have it your way,' chuckled the handyman. 'Mickey's not here to help, anyway. He's here to tell. That tracker … well, it's not tracking anymore. Switched off most probably. As for the suitcase, Mickey doesn't know what's happened to that—'

'I do,' said Candy, scampering across the rug. 'It's over here … and here … and here … and here …'

She was right. Once Poppy had cut the suitcase to shreds its remains had been cast all over the Great Room as we searched for the secret tunnel.

'Don't think this will be going on holiday anytime soon,' remarked Candy, as she held up the handle and very little else.

A snigger from Mickey the Fix was enough to grab their attention. 'If the spy's found the tracker, then he'll probably be long gone by now,' the handyman said, trying not to laugh.

'Maybe you should follow his lead,' suggested Frankie. 'This room ain't big enough for the three of us. Why don't you go and play in the garden?'

'Could do,' the handyman smirked. At the same time he gestured towards the exit. 'Shall we leave together? You … you … and Mickey the Fix. Ladies first …'

'Not likely,' insisted Candy, pushing the handyman in the back.

A beaming Mickey the Fix took one last look around before he finally departed the Great Room.

Wary of being overheard, Frankie left it a moment or two before he spoke again. 'He can go one way and we'll go the other,' he said quietly. 'We'll find the kid before anybody else and then hot-tail it out of this dingy old dump. We'll be halfway home before anybody even realises. And then we'll collect our prize.'

'That sounds like a mighty fine idea,' gushed Candy.

I turned away as she leant in for a kiss. The two of them made a horrible squelching sound (think plunger trying to clear a blocked drain) before Candy grabbed Frankie by the hand and led him out of the room in search of yours truly.

They had gone.

Pushing past the guard, I scrambled out of the fireplace and turned towards the suit of armour. Poppy had pressed the tip of the sword, but, even after all the years it had spent on display, it still looked much sharper than I would've liked.

Ouch!

I touched it once, but nothing happened. I could hear voices. No, just a voice. And a barking dog.

Ouch!

I touched it again and this time the door in the wall began to slowly open. I waited until the gap was at least Hugo-sized before I hurried inside, stopping only to touch the tip for a third (and hopefully final) time. The door came to a sudden halt and then began to close. That was when I saw him.

Mr Bones.

He was on all fours, sniffing the floor as he bounded into the Great Room. He seemed to have detected a scent. And there was only one scent in there that he could have detected.

And that was mine.

Driven by a thirst for revenge, Mr Bones made his way towards the fireplace. If his eyes drifted towards the suit of armour then he would see the secret tunnel.

And that meant he would see me.

The door was closing, but it wasn't closing fast enough. Frozen to the spot, I watched as the human hound edged closer to where I was stood. He came to a sudden halt as he reached the fireplace and pressed his nose up to the fireguard. I could barely breathe now. He was so close I could practically touch him.

And then he was even closer. Creeping to one side, Mr Bones turned his attention to the suit of armour. There was nothing I could do now. If he looked up I was dog food.

Not if … when!

My worst fears came true as Mr Bones lifted his head … we locked eyes … and … and … and the door to the secret tunnel finally closed.

A demented Mr Bones began to scratch wildly at the wall, but there was no way he could get inside. Not unless he touched the tip of the sword, and who would ever think of doing that? Yes, okay, Poppy did. But she was at least ten times smarter than a man who pretended to be a dog. Not to mention every other member of the Undesirable Eight put together.

With no wish to hang around a moment longer, I moved away from the door and tried to get my bearings. The tunnel was darker than dark and I couldn't see much beyond my own eyebrows. Lifting my arms, I was surprised to find that I didn't have to reach far before I touched the wall on either side of me. It was cold and hard and uncomfortably close. I did the exact same thing above my head and felt the ceiling. Okay, so I still couldn't see much, but at least I now knew how big the tunnel was.

Not very.

I kept my knees bent and my shoulders hunched as I tried to move my feet. Half a dozen steps later I stopped.

'Poppy?' I whispered. 'Where are you?'

I listened carefully, but there was no reply. It left me with no other choice but to continue to shuffle forwards like a nervous ice-skater on very thin ice. Not only was the tunnel beginning to slope downwards, but it also seemed to be getting darker. With nothing to see and no way to see it, every step filled me with dread. For all I knew I was about to fall into some kind of hole. Or just a hole. That was even worse.

I hadn't gone far when I came to another halt.

'Poppy?' This time it was less of a whisper and more of a cry. I was starting to panic. 'Where are … urrggghhhh!'

I was stopped mid-sentence as a hand covered my mouth. Next thing I knew I was being dragged backwards, deeper and deeper in to the darkness.

That's what happens when you linger for too long in a secret tunnel.

You get pounced on.

29.'I HIT HIM! I HIT HIM!'

I had a plan of attack.

A plan that I was about to put into action. Or should that be attack-tion?

Concentrate, Hugo. This is serious.

I lifted my foot and raised my elbow, all set to strike out against my mystery man-handler when I heard a voice in my ear.

'Don't do that, Hugo!'

Only one person called me Hugo.

'It's me.'

Me was Poppy.

'Don't make a sound,' she said. 'You don't want them to hear you in the Great Room, do you?' I doubted Poppy could see me shaking my head in the darkness, but that didn't stop her from removing her hand from my mouth. 'I wondered when you were going to show up,' she continued, her voice barely a whisper. 'We need to move fast and get out of this tunnel as quickly as possible. Follow me and try not to do anything foolish.'

Foolish? Who? Me? As if I would …

I had no idea how long the tunnel was and no intention of asking Poppy if she knew as we set off into the gloom. Imagine if she told me it was three or four miles. Or even thirty-four for that matter. The thought of it was enough to make me almost fall over. Or maybe I would've just fallen over anyway. It does happen from time to time.

'You don't think the Undesirable Eight will find us down here, do you?' I asked, wiping the cobwebs from my face.

'Hopefully not,' replied Poppy. 'I mean, half of them wouldn't even fit in the tunnel to begin with. They'd get stuck. And, besides, we've moved too far along it now for them to catch up with us. I wouldn't be surprised if we're nearly at the end.'

I liked the sound of that. I liked it even more when the tunnel sloped upwards and Poppy walked straight into a solid stone wall. I, naturally, did much the same thing and walked straight into Poppy.

'Now … with any luck … there should be … ah, there it is,' she remarked, pointing at a hatch in the ceiling. 'I just need a little assistance if you're feeling strong enough.'

'Do you really need to ask?' I sighed. Okay, so I wasn't really feeling that strong if I'm being honest, but that didn't stop me from placing my hands on the hatch. 'Ready when you are, Pops.'

We worked together and pushed hard. I had a bad feeling the hatch might have jammed shut over time, but I was wrong. Instead, it held firm for barely a second before, one loud *creak* later, it flew to one side. Without missing a beat, Poppy hauled herself up through the opening until she had vanished from view. I followed her lead and found myself in what appeared to be a rickety old barn with no windows. At first glance the wooden walls that surrounded us appeared to have rotted away over time, whilst the low ceiling was sagging in the middle, almost as if it could collapse at any moment. There were a number of large barrels in one corner, but aside from that the barn was empty.

'These look interesting,' I said, resting a hand on one of the barrels.

'I wouldn't touch those if I was you,' replied Poppy. 'They're oil barrels. Highly dangerous in the wrong hands. We used them to heat the house when I was young, but that's not necessary anymore. Not since … you know … my parents …' Keen to end that particular conversation, Poppy moved swiftly across the barn so she could listen at the door. 'If we hide in here for too long we'll get caught,' she remarked. 'That's why I'll leave first and head straight for the Mini. Hopefully, I can get away without being spotted. Give me a minute and then it's your turn. I'll meet you at the foot of the garden, by the back fence that separates Wildheart Hall from the road.' Poppy took a moment to clean her glasses. 'I don't want us to split up, but it's probably for the best,' she shrugged. 'They're not after me, remember. Only you.'

'Thanks for reminding me,' I grumbled.

Ever so gently, Poppy opened the door to the barn and peeked outside.

'All clear,' she said quietly. 'I'll leave now whilst the Undesirable Eight are still in the house. Good luck, Hugo.'

'Straight back at you.' I wanted to say something else. Something to inspire her. Something to send her on her way with a spring in her step and a smile on her face. Unfortunately, I never got the chance because, by the time I had opened my mouth and the words had formed on my tongue, Poppy had gone.

I began to count. One minute. That's sixty seconds to you and me. At least, it was the last time I looked. Maybe it had changed since then and nobody had bothered to tell me.

It didn't take long for me to reach the magic number (about sixty seconds as it turns out. Who would've thought that?) I gave it another five for good measure and then pressed my ear to the door. As far as I could tell there was nothing going on outside that would cause me any distress. By that I mean shouts and screams. Gunshots and explosions. You know, all the bad stuff.

I steadied my nerves and opened the door. The first thing that struck me was how far I was from Wildheart Hall. About the length of a football pitch at a guess. Even from that distance the house still seemed huge, though. My eyes dropped a little lower and I spotted a random cluster of furniture and decorative ornaments dotted about the garden, not to mention three more water fountains as impressive as the one I had passed in the driveway. As expected, Poppy was nowhere to be seen.

But somebody else was.

No, make that *five* somebody elses.

Sneezing Stan, Wheezing Wally, Captain Olga Kartoffel and Mickey the Fix were all facing towards the house as they searched for yours truly. They hadn't seen me. I was sure of it.

But the fifth *somebody else* most certainly had.

Up until that moment, Candy Gloss had been skipping towards the barn without a care in the world. Not now, though. Now she had stopped. For the briefest of moments we just stared at each other like two startled rabbits caught in the headlights. Then the moment passed and Candy pulled something from her dress.

Something short and stubby. Something dangerous.

Something like a gun.

I slammed the door shut and fell back into the barn as Candy fired off a single shot. To my horror, the bullet passed through the wall and then out the other side before I could even duck my head.

'I hit him! I hit him!' squealed Candy. She followed that up by firing off five more shots in quick succession. Two of them didn't even reach the barn, whilst two more passed through the rotting walls unhindered.

One, however, hit its target.

No, not me, but a target nevertheless. One of the oil barrels to be precise.

I froze as the bullet ripped a hole in its side and then never came out.

I soon defrosted, though, when the barrel burst into flames.

Scrambling across the floor, I covered my face as the heat hit me with a powerful *whoosh*. I didn't need to look to know that the fire was spreading quickly. Up the walls and over the ceiling. I needed to get out of there and fast. That was obvious. But how could I?

I was trapped inside a burning barn with over half of the Undesirable Eight waiting for me to leave. I had nowhere to go and nowhere to hide.

Which basically meant I had no chance of survival.

Fact.

30.'DID I DO SOMETHING WRONG?'

The wooden barn was going to burn down.

That much was true.

It was also true that if I tried to escape through the door, then Candy Gloss, or perhaps one of the other less trigger-happy undesirables, would fire at me. They might even hit me. They might even …

No, don't go there, Hugo. Let's go somewhere else entirely.

Because that was my plan. To go somewhere else entirely. Somewhere that no one could see me.

I know what you're thinking, but you're wrong. Yes, I could've used the secret tunnel, but then what would be the point in that? Best case scenario, I would find myself stuck in the darkness, halfway between Mr Bones on one side and a raging fire on the other. I'd be trapped. Again. And there's only so many times a spy like me can find himself trapped before it starts to become really rather boring.

Instead, I clambered to my feet and took a running jump at one of the wooden panels at the rear of the barn. I tried to choose wisely, picking the one that looked weakest and, therefore, unable to take my weight. It was just a guess, though. Nothing more. For all I knew it might hold firm and I'd be back where I started.

It was make or break time ... because if the panel didn't break there was no way I'd be making it out of there alive.

I closed my eyes as I hit the wall shoulder first. Just for a moment I panicked. The wood wasn't as weak as I had hoped. But it wasn't that strong either. Splintering around me, it soon gave way under the pressure and I emerged out the other side. I staggered forward as a series of sharp pains shot up and down my body. Somehow, I managed to keep my balance.

I had to keep moving.

Poppy had told me to make my way towards the fence at the foot of the garden so that was what I did. Using the blazing barn as cover, I began to hobble in the opposite direction to Wildheart Hall. I wanted to run, but that wasn't possible. Not yet, anyway.

I hadn't hobbled far when I heard a shout from behind me.

'What have you done?'

That was Mr Skinner. I'd recognise his growl anywhere.

Fearful of being spotted out in the open, I ducked down behind a bird bath so I could catch my breath. Safely hidden, I watched as every last member of the Undesirable Eight gathered around the barn, careful to keep their distance in case the flames spread towards them.

'I saw the kid and I shot the kid.' Candy stopped

bouncing up and down and straightened her wedding dress. 'Did I do something wrong?' she asked innocently.

'Something wrong?' Mr Skinner snatched the gun from Candy's grasp and tossed it over his shoulder. 'Of course you've done something wrong,' he yelled. 'A *lot* wrong. That maggot was not to be harmed. Under any circumstances. So, what did you go and do? Oh, you just killed him. That's all. Congratulations. The hunt for Hugo Dare is over … and it's all your fault!'

'Hey, don't be like that,' said Frankie, stepping between the two of them. 'Accidents do happen from time to time …'

'This was no accident,' argued Captain Kartoffel.

'Well, it was hardly deliberate,' pleaded Candy. 'I'm not completely crazy.'

'Who told you that?' laughed Mickey the Fix.

'I just wanted to fire the gun,' Candy insisted. 'Not blow the blooming barn up!'

A seething Mr Skinner slapped his metal leg in anger. 'We have failed,' he said grumpily. 'There are no winners here. Just losers.'

'Nothing new there then,' muttered Frankie. With that, he tucked his arm under Candy's and pulled her towards him. 'Now, if it's all the same to you guys, I think me and my precious pumpkin here will bid you a fond farewell and skedaddle. No offence, but we're sick of hanging around with you deadbeats …'

'Think again.' The tone of Mr Skinner's voice seemed to rouse Mr Bones, who began to strain against his lead. 'You're not going anywhere.'

Wheezing Wally and Sneezing Stan took this as their cue to step forward, whilst a grinning Mickey the Fix removed his hammer from under his armpit.

'Nobody leaves,' remarked Captain Kartoffel.

Except for me. I had seen enough, heard enough and, most definitely, had enough. Stepping out from behind the bird bath, I stayed in the shadows as I crept carefully through the grounds of Wildheart Hall. I had a feeling that things were going to get particularly messy behind me. Messy *and* bloody. Not a particularly pleasant combination, but one that still brought a smile to my face as I edged closer to safety.

With the fence in sight, I took one last look over my shoulder before I left Wildheart Hall behind me. The barn was still ablaze as the Undesirable Eight continued to scuffle and scrap amongst themselves. Candy Gloss had climbed onto Mr Skinner's back, Frankie Fingertips was struggling to keep both Mickey the Fix and Captain Kartoffel at arm's length, whilst Mr Bones was snapping at the sunglasses of Sneezing Stan and Wheezing Wally. It was absolute bedlam. A complete disaster zone. And I loved it.

I leapt over the fence at the exact same moment as the Mini appeared beside me. Before it had even skidded to a halt, I yanked open the door and dived into the back.

'What happened?' cried Poppy from the driver's seat. 'I saw the barn go up in flames. I thought you might be still inside it.'

'I was,' I admitted, 'and then I wasn't. Not that the Undesirable Eight know that. They all think I'm dead.'

'Do they really?' Poppy stamped down on the accelerator and the Mini shot forward. 'That's probably worth remembering,' she muttered under her breath. 'Rest in peace, Hugo Dare. It's been nice knowing you.'

31.'THAT'S THE BEST NEWS I'VE HEARD ALL DAY.'

Poppy drove me to The Impossible Pizza takeaway.

That was something of a surprise. I was even more surprised to find that the Big Cheese was there waiting for us by the time we had made our way down to the SICK Bucket.

'Young Dare,' he hollered. 'You're still alive. That's an unexpected bonus.'

'Thank you, sir,' I said.

'Don't thank me – thank Poppy,' the Big Cheese roared. 'I told you she was the best personal assistant I've ever had. And now she's only gone and proved it. Bravo, Miss Wildheart. The congratulations are all yours.'

Poppy began to blush. 'There's no need, sir ... really ... I'm sure anybody would've done what I did—'

'I wouldn't,' boomed the Big Cheese. 'Not on your nelly. No way whatsoever. I would've just left young Dare to fend for himself.'

Poppy quickly changed the subject before I got too

offended. 'What now, sir?' she asked.

'Now it's story time.' With that, the Big Cheese wandered into his Pantry, sat down on the carpet and crossed his legs. 'I want you to tell me everything, young Dare,' he demanded. 'From the very beginning. And make it exciting.'

I took a deep breath, opened my mouth and let it all flood out. I got a few things mixed up along the way, and Poppy had to correct me in places, but by the time I had finished even I was shocked at how terrible the last few days had been.

'So … this Undesirable Eight as they like to call themselves … they all think you're dead, right?' remarked the Big Cheese, a little too cheerfully for my liking.

'That's correct, sir,' I nodded.

'Splendid.' The Big Cheese clapped his hands together in delight. 'That's the best news I've heard in days.'

I screwed up my face. 'Is it, sir?'

'Indeed.' I thought the Big Cheese might try and explain himself, but all he did was pass me a large rectangular box. 'Pizza, young Dare? Impossible Rita cooked it last Wednesday so it'll be as cold as icicles by now. Don't let that put you off, though.'

I didn't. Opening the box, I removed a couple of slices, both of which looked like no other pizza I had ever seen before. 'What are the toppings, sir?'

'Watermelon and walnut,' announced the Big Cheese proudly. 'Impossible Rita took my advice onboard and decided to experiment with some new ingredients. Admittedly, this particular pizza does fail somewhat tragically in the flavour department, but I, for one, won't hold it against her. Besides, there's no way that *you'll* notice how bad it tastes, young Dare? Not now that you're … dead!'

I screwed up my face for a second time. 'You do know that I'm not really dead, don't you, sir?'

'I think so,' replied the Big Cheese, studying me closely. 'It's just hard to tell sometimes. Right, if we're all done here …'

I watched as the Chief of SICK uncrossed his legs and climbed (at the fourth attempt) to his feet.

'Going somewhere, sir?' I asked.

'Home,' the Big Cheese replied. 'It's late. Or is it early? Both probably. And before you ask, no, you can't come with me. You can, however, stay here in the SICK Bucket and sleep in my Pantry. I'm nice like that. You can even use an empty pizza box or two as a cardboard blanket to keep yourself warm.'

Poppy shifted towards the exit. 'Would you like me to see you out, sir?'

'Not yet,' insisted the Big Cheese. 'I've got a few phone calls to make first, one of which is to young Dare's parents. You don't think they'll be too upset when I tell them the bad news, do you? Death by blazing barn isn't the best way to go.' The Big Cheese began to laugh. 'Only joking,' he barked. 'I'll tell them the truth. It can be our little secret. The other phone call I have to make is to Father O'Garble at the Pearly Gates Cemetery. I've got a funeral to arrange at very short notice. I'm aiming for later on this morning.

Tricky, but not impossible. About eleven o'clock would be perfect. Get it done and dusted in time for lunch.' The Big Cheese stopped in the doorway and pointed straight at me. 'I don't need to tell you whose funeral I'm talking about, do I, young Dare?'

With that, the Chief of SICK stomped out of the Pantry, leaving me staring at Poppy in a state of bewilderment. 'Did he really just say that?'

The look on Poppy's face seemed to suggest he had.

'The Big Cheese is arranging my funeral,' I moaned. 'My *fake* funeral. He wants me to carry on pretending I'm dead. And then what? Do you think that will finally put a stop to things?'

'Maybe … maybe not,' shrugged Poppy. 'But I do know something. However much you like pizza, there's no way you can hide in here for the rest of your life. Before long you'll have to leave and then what? If you get spotted out in the open it'll all start again. The Undesirable Eight will be back on the hunt.' Poppy stopped to think. 'We need to end this once and for all,' she said eventually. 'We shouldn't run and hide – we should stand our ground and fight.'

To my surprise, Poppy opened her hand and showed me the tracker that she had removed from the suitcase. 'What are you thinking?' I asked warily.

'I'm thinking you should try and get some sleep,' remarked Poppy, returning the tracker to her pocket. 'And so should I. I'll come back and see you tomorrow. We don't want you getting bored now, do we?'

'Definitely not.' I watched as Poppy followed the Big

Cheese out of the Pantry. The two of them spoke for a moment and then left the SICK Bucket together. All alone, I rolled under the table and closed my eyes. I was absolutely exhausted after everything that had happened, but my mind was still wide awake. One thought in particular refused to go away. Despite what Poppy had just said, I had no intention of getting bored the next day. No, I had a busy morning planned.

A busy morning that would lead me all the way to the Pearly Gates Cemetery.

I woke exactly five hours and thirty-seven minutes later. Pushing aside my empty pizza box blanket, I jumped to my feet and then regretted it instantly as my back cried out in agony and my head began to spin. Turns out sleeping on the floor isn't that comfortable, after all. Who would've thought that?

Shuffling out of the Big Cheese's Pantry, I took a slight detour to Poppy's desk when something colourful caught my eye. It was a note on yellow paper.

Good morning, Hugo.
Meet me at midday in the Bulging Bellyful.
The Big Cheese doesn't know it yet,
but I've got something up my sleeve.
All will be revealed in due course.
See you soon, Poppy.
P.S. don't forget to lock the door on your way out.

I read the note twice before I scrunched it up and flicked it into the nearest wastepaper bin. Midday. Also known as twelve o'clock. The time was just gone ten in the morning so I had slightly less than two hours to do what had to be done.

Starting with a disguise.

I searched every drawer and filing cabinet I could find until I stumbled upon what I was (hardly) looking for. There were four things in total. A bright orange baseball cap. A pair of plastic reading glasses. A red marker pen. And a floppy rubber caterpillar.

I put the baseball cap on backwards and perched the glasses on the end of my nose. I found a mirror after that and used the pen to dab some freckles onto my cheeks. So far, so good. My disguise was progressing well. It was taking shape.

And then I picked up the caterpillar.

I don't know why I thought it'd be a good idea to stick it under my chin and pretend it was a beard, but that was what I did. Still, it was too late to change it now. Why? Because I'd used fast-sticking super glue to secure it in place. Never mind. Now wasn't the time to worry about how I was going to remove it. No, I'd save that for later. Or maybe I wouldn't. Maybe I'd just leave the caterpillar there forever.

Disguise in place, I grabbed one more slice of cold pizza and then set off up the rubbish chute. It took me a while but I finally emerged in The Impossible Pizza. Without breaking stride, I marched across the length of the takeaway and headed outside, stopping only to lock the door behind me and push the key back through the letterbox.

Then I was off, hurrying along the pavement, picking up speed with every step.

Destination: the Pearly Gates Cemetery.

The last thing I wanted was to be late for my own funeral.

32.'THERE'S ALWAYS
A NEXT TIME.'

As feared, my funeral had already started by the time I had arrived at the Pearly Gates Cemetery.

Without a second to spare, I hurried towards the best hiding place I could find and began to climb.

It was a tree in case you're wondering.

I stopped about three branches up and got comfortable. Slowly, in case I accidentally lost my balance and fell out, I leant forward and looked out over the grounds of the cemetery.

Does any of this sound familiar? Because it should do. This was where my story began. In the prologue. Can you remember that far back? No, me neither. Just give me a moment or two and I'll try and claw back the memories.

Right, I'm ready when you are …

I waited until the coffin had been lowered into the open grave before I shifted my gaze to those in attendance. Aside from the stumbling, mumbling Father O'Garble (who, despite being there to oversee things, always seemed to be looking in the wrong direction), there were only three other people mourning my sorry demise. One was my mother, one was my father and the other was the Big Cheese.

Aside from Poppy, they were the only other people who knew that I wasn't really dead.

I watched as my mother, Doreen, removed a crusty, old tissue from somewhere up her sleeve and pressed it to her nose. The nasally blast that followed was both ridiculously loud and unnecessarily snotty. Never one to be outdone, my father, Dirk, howled out loud like a wolf in the wild before falling dramatically to his knees and burying his face in a molehill. Or maybe it was a huge pile of manure. It was hard to tell from where I was perched.

Either way, one thing was clear. No one would ever miss me that much. Not even my own parents. So don't overdo it please.

I looked past my own funeral to the other side of the cemetery. There was a wire fence that ran around the perimeter and beyond that, an ugly crowd lurking in the shadows. Even from a distance I recognised the faces. Mr Skinner and Mr Bones. Frankie Fingertips and Candy Gloss. Sneezing Stan and Wheezing Wally. Captain Olga Kartoffel and Mickey the Fix. The Undesirable Eight were out in force and yet not one of them had turned up to bid me a fond farewell. No, they were only there for confirmation. They needed to know that I had died. And that's exactly what was happening now. They could see it with their own eyes.

RIP Hugo Dare.

The service was coming to an end and there was no need

for me to hang around a moment longer. Not unless I wanted to be spotted. And nobody wants to be spotted halfway up a tree on the day of their own funeral.

Scrambling down the trunk, I quickly checked that the coast was clear before I made an even quicker getaway. Maybe the Big Cheese's plan had worked. Maybe we really had convinced the Undesirable Eight that I was as dead as a dinosaur.

I had almost left the Pearly Gates Cemetery well and truly behind me when I heard a voice. It was coming from above. No, not up a tree. That was my trick.

'Wotcha', Stinky.'

I stopped suddenly. There was a girl sat on top of the wall beside the exit. She looked familiar. More than familiar, in fact. *Worryingly* familiar …

No way. Surely not. It couldn't be her. Not in a million years.

Oh. My mistake.

It could and it was.

Her name was Fatale De'Ath … and she was trouble!

Let me explain. Fatale and I had history. The last time we had met I had tried to rescue her from Elbow's End … even though she didn't need rescuing! She could have told me that herself, of course, but chose not to. No, to her it was just a bit of fun. A joke. In my mind, however, it was one of the most perilous missions I had ever undertaken. Thankfully, I got out of there in one piece … but only by the skin of my teeth. And that's why I had no wish to rescue Fatale (or even see her for that matter) ever again.

Oh, one last thing before I crack on with the story. It's probably worth mentioning that Fatale is also Deadly De'Ath's daughter. Yes, that does seem quite important in hindsight. Still, at least you know now.

Back to the Pearly Gates Cemetery and my natural reaction was to turn and run. My natural reaction, however, didn't react quick enough and I forgot to move.

'Fancy seeing you here,' remarked Fatale. 'No, wait! Of course you're here. It's your funeral, after all. Boo-hoo. So sad. Except ... it's not, is it? Sad, I mean. Because you're still alive. I can see that with my own eyes. It's ... it's ... it's ... it's a miracle!'

I screwed up my face. And then screwed it up some more because one screw just wasn't enough.

'Nice disguise, by the way,' Fatale continued. 'I especially like the freckles. I'm not so sure about the caterpillar, though. Bit weird.'

'You'd know,' I snapped back at her. Without thinking, I tried to remove my disguise and toss it in the nearest rubbish bin. The freckles, however, weren't so easy to shift. 'Now, is that it or is there anything else?' I asked bluntly. 'Because I really shouldn't—'

'Come with me,' blurted out Fatale. With that, she jumped down from the wall and landed beside me. She was dressed in black from head to toe. Quite unusual for her really. Especially seeing as I'd only ever known her to wear pink.

I was all set to walk away when Fatale grabbed me by the arm. 'Not polite enough for you, eh, Stinky?' she said.

'Okay, let me try again. Please, oh pretty please, will you do me the honour of following me in a direction of my choosing, thank you kindly and all that nonsense?' Fatale snatched a breath. 'How was that? Any good?'

'No,' I said, pushing her to one side.

Fatale slapped a hand against her forehead. 'Now, I'm really confused,' she moaned. 'Is that, no, I'm not asking politely enough, or is it—?'

'No, I won't come with you,' I said firmly. I followed that up by barging past her as I finally exited the cemetery. I had already wasted far too much time talking. My funeral would be over by now and the last thing I wanted was to be seen out on the streets.

'Why not?' asked Fatale, her silvery-white pigtails flapping up and down as she followed me along the pavement. 'What's wrong with me?'

'Wow!' I cried. 'Where to begin? You're dangerous … and violent … and strange … and—'

'That's a list of all my good points,' smirked Fatale, finishing my sentence. 'Now, what's wrong with me?'

I tried to speed up, but I couldn't quite shake her off. 'Oh, and your father just happens to be Deadly De'Ath,' I said matter-of-factly. 'Also known as Crooked Elbow's number one criminal mastermind.'

'Okay, there's no need to rub it in,' moaned Fatale. 'You are right, though. That is quite annoying. Still, he's perfectly harmless when you get to know him.'

'I don't want to get to know him,' I insisted.

'No, but he'd like to get to know you,' muttered Fatale to

herself. 'Okay, Stinky, I can see why you might be a little jumpy-jumpy. We haven't seen each other for a while … and I did lie to you … a lot … and almost got you killed … several times … but that's all in the past. I've changed. This is the new me. I'm a good girl now.' Stepping in front of me, Fatale put her hands on my chest and stopped me from walking. 'There's no point trying to argue with me,' she said smugly. 'I always get my way. That's a fact. I know it, you know it—'

'I don't know that at all,' I replied stubbornly.

'You do now,' grinned Fatale. 'I've just told you. So, let's go. There's somewhere I want to take you …'

Fatale tried to grab me by the arm again, but this time I was ready. Stepping to one side, I dodged her completely and she almost fell over. By the time she had regained her balance, I was already on the move.

'Have it your way,' Fatale called out, refusing to give chase. 'It's your choice, I suppose, although next time you might not be so lucky.'

'There won't be a next time,' I shouted back at her.

'There's always a next time,' declared Fatale. 'See you soon, Stinky. *Very* soon.'

I was just about to turn a corner when the urge became too great and I glanced back over my shoulder. Oddly enough, Fatale De'Ath didn't seem overly concerned that I had left her behind. If anything, she looked happy. Happy to see me off with a friendly smile and a casual wave of her hand.

And that probably explains why I started to run the moment I was out of sight.

33.'I WON'T LEAVE
WITHOUT A STRUGGLE.'

I ran all the way to the Bulging Bellyful.

I was pretty sure that Fatale De'Ath hadn't followed me. At least eighty-three per-cent certain. The other seventeen per-cent, however, expected her to pop up at any moment, grinning from ear to ear, begging me to go with her. That was never going to happen, though. Even the thought of it was enough to make me dive for cover the moment I burst into the café. I waited a while and then crawled over to the window so I could peek through the grimy glass. As far as I could tell, there was no sign of Deadly De'Ath's dastardly daughter. Ten … twenty … thirty-one seconds later and nothing had changed. To my relief, Fatale was still nowhere to be seen.

'I'm behind you!'

I leapt up off the floor and spun around at the same time. You can try it if you like. It's not as easy as it sounds. Somehow, I stayed on my feet, but then instantly regretted it when I crashed straight into Grot. For the second time

207

that weekend we almost brushed lips.

Whoa! Don't look at me like that. It's not my fault.

As usual, the oafish owner of the Bulging Bellyful was stood far too close for comfort (although nine miles in the opposite direction was still too close so I can hardly blame her for that). More worrying perhaps was the fact that Grot had managed to creep up on me unnoticed. I say worrying because I should really have got a whiff of her earlier. Like a cross between crusty toenails on an unwashed foot and chunks of earwax soaked in a dog bowl, the stench that Grot gave off was powerfully pungent to say the least. Fearful for my nostrils, I took a step to my right … and then five more steps after that. The stench wasn't quite so strong over there.

The view, however, was horrendous.

Don't get me wrong; the Bulging Bellyful was hardly the cleanliest of cafés. But that still didn't explain the sight that greeted me now.

'What's happened?' I spluttered.

'Ya happened,' replied Grot, pointing a knobbly finger at me. 'Ya and those rotten rogues and wrong 'uns that followed ya in. Ya turned the Bulgin' Bellyful into a right mucky mess, didn't ya?'

I suppose she had a point. Except it wasn't strictly true, was it? Because this had nothing to do with me. What's that? It did? Well, maybe a little. Admittedly, I had started the whole thing off, but then how was I to know that the Undesirable Eight would declare all-out war on each other and turn it into a furious food fight? That same food was now everywhere I looked. Across every surface and up the walls. Hanging from the ceiling and smeared across the floor. This would take some cleaning, make no mistake.

And that's when I remembered.

I had promised to come back and help tidy up. And that was something that Grot wasn't prepared to let me forget.

'Ya promised ya'd come back and help tidy up,' she said, repeating my thoughts word for word.

I screwed up my face. 'And … here I am.'

'"Course ya are.' Grot reached over and punched me on the arm. 'That's why yer ma favourite customer,' she grinned. 'Where d'ya wanna' start?'

I was still trying to think of a good excuse when the door to the Bulging Bellyful flew open and in marched Poppy. She spotted the mess and began to frown. Then she spotted me and the frown only intensified.

'You start over there and I'll join you in a moment,' I said, pointing at the furthest corner. 'I've just got to speak to my friend first.'

This seemed to satisfy Grot who shuffled away without another word. A second later and Poppy had taken her place.

'Sit down, Hugo,' she said, gesturing towards the nearest table. 'We haven't got long.'

'Shame,' I muttered. 'The longer the better as far as I'm concerned. Then I won't have to get scrubbing.'

I pulled up a chair and sat down. Poppy, however, preferred to stand. 'Take this,' she said, handing me the tracker that she had removed from the suitcase. 'Hide it somewhere that nobody can find it.'

I did as she said and stuffed it down the front of my

trousers. 'Perfectly safe,' I remarked. 'Now, what did you want to see me about?'

Poppy opened her mouth to speak, but nothing came out. By the look on her face, she seemed to be struggling with something. Or maybe she just needed the toilet. Either way, it was time to get to the bottom of things.

'What's wrong?' I asked. 'And don't say nothing because that's not true. There's something. I can tell.'

'I've got to go.' Shifting awkwardly on the spot, Poppy glanced over at the door. 'You, however, can't.'

'I can't what?' I shrugged.

'Go,' insisted Poppy. 'You have to stay … stay here … don't go anywhere else.'

'Really?' I moaned. 'Why am I being punished?'

'You're not.' Poppy closed her eyes, shook her head and bit down on her lip. It was so obvious that there was something wrong that it may as well have been scrawled across her forehead (it wasn't in case you're wondering. I did look, though. Just to be certain.) 'You do trust me, don't you, Hugo?' she asked.

I nodded, but the tone of her voice made my skin prickle.

'Good,' sighed Poppy. Turning her back on me, she hurried towards the door. 'Everything will work out fine in the end. I'm sure of it.'

I watched her leave before I switched my attention back to Grot. Armed with a mop and bucket, she appeared to be fighting a losing battle with a particularly stubborn splodge that had stuck to the floor. Whether I liked it or not, she needed help (and, worst luck, a lot of it).

Still, it wasn't as if I had anything else to do, was it? Not now I was officially dead and buried.

I pushed back my chair and stood up. 'Have you got any rubber gloves?' I asked.

Looking up from the splodge, Grot was about to speak when a curious change came over her. Not only did her eyes bulge out of their sockets, but her mouth fell open and thin streams of dribble began to roll off the end of her chin.

'No disrespect, but that's one face I'd rather not see again,' I laughed. 'What's wrong? Anyone would think you'd seen a ghost.'

'Worse than any ghost,' mumbled Grot, pointing over my head.

I followed her finger and saw two men in the entrance to the Bulging Bellyful.

No, make that one man and his dog.

'This is an unexpected surprise,' remarked Mr Skinner. 'It was a good trick, but you don't look very dead to me. That, however, may be about to change …'

'Get out of ma café!' squealed Grot from behind her mop.

'If only,' grumbled Skinner. 'Unfortunately, I can't. Not without the maggot.'

'Dream on, you big lump,' I cried. 'I'm not going anywhere with you and your flea-ridden friend.'

'Then we have a problem.' Lifting his metal leg, Mr Skinner took several clunky strides into the café. Mr Bones followed. He was walking on all fours. And off his lead. On Skinner's word, he would attack. And I hardly need to remind you who would be the focus of his anger.

As far as I could tell, I had two choices. Fight or flight? It wasn't a difficult decision. Especially with no passing aeroplanes to carry me to safety.

Turning away from Mr Skinner, I held out my hands and mouthed a single word. 'Mop.'

A gormless Grot gazed at me in confusion before she finally put two and two together and threw the mop across the length of the café. I caught it with one hand before moving swiftly behind the nearest table. Now I had both a weapon and a shield. Or as good as.

'I won't leave without a struggle,' I said defiantly.

'I wouldn't have expected anything less,' shrugged Skinner. 'It's a struggle that will end badly, though.'

And with that, Mr Bones was off and running. I tensed up as he leapt into the air and landed on the table. With his eyes wide with rage, he was about to pounce when I turned the mop on its side and rammed it between his jaws. Bones howled in horror, but it wasn't enough to make him back away.

Not that I wanted him to.

Letting go of the mop, I placed both hands under the table and began to tip it backwards until it eventually toppled over. As I hoped, Bones fell off first and the table rolled on top of him.

'Do we really have to do this?' moaned Skinner.

He was talking to me, but I was far too busy grabbing the mop and running towards him to listen. We were about to collide when I fell to my knees and slid along the floor. I was still on the move when I swung the mop. I was aiming for Skinner's ankle.

Clang.

Oh. That didn't sound very painful.

'Good shot,' muttered Skinner, shaking his head at me. 'That was my metal leg, though. You should probably have hit the other one.'

'Thanks for the advice.' Switching hands, I swung the mop and did exactly what Skinner suggested. I hit his other leg.

Thunk.

Ah, that was better.

Mr Skinner's first reaction was to howl like his hairy partner. His second, however, was to haul me into the air by the lapels of my tuxedo.

'Why do you always insist on making things so hard for yourself?' he growled.

'I'm just awkward, I guess.' Lifting the mop between us, I twirled it once and then rubbed the wet end all over Skinner's face. When I pulled it away, he was covered in all the lumpy bits of food that Grot had scraped up off the floor. They were plastered to his lips. Poking out of his ears. Disappearing up his nostrils. And, perhaps most conveniently of all, sticking to his eyeballs.

'What have you done?' A panic-stricken Mr Skinner had little choice but to let go of me so he could wipe the food from his face. I landed on both feet, but chose to stay low as I scrambled between his legs rather than run around him.

The exit was straight ahead of me.

Run, Hugo. Run.

I was almost there when two hands pushed me in the back and I fell forward. I was about to go again when the hands moved quickly and pinned me to the floor. And that was when I realised they weren't hands at all, but paws. It was Mr Bones. I tried to shrug him off and his weight shifted to one side. Maybe I still had a chance.

A sharp, stinging pain in my neck, however, seemed to suggest otherwise.

Mr Bones let go and I rolled onto my back. The first thing I saw was Mr Skinner. He was crouched over me with something in his hand. A syringe.

'Sorry if that hurt,' he said, not sorry in the slightest.

I was about to speak when my mouth went numb and my eyes glazed over.

'You feel dizzy, don't you?' Mr Skinner couldn't help but smile. 'Good. That is normal. Any moment now you will fall asleep. That is normal, too. Don't try and fight it. Fighting it will only make things worse.'

Naturally, I ignored him. But it was no use.

'Sleep tight, Maggot,' whispered Skinner, as my eyes began to close. 'It's *not* been nice knowing you.'

34.'WHY HAVE YOU BROUGHT ME HERE?'

'Stinky!'

I wasn't awake. That was obvious. This had to be a dream.

'Stinky!'

No. Stop it. There was only one person who called me Stinky. And she couldn't be here. Not again. Not in real life. In my nightmares perhaps.

'Stinky!'

Something prodded me in the side of the head. Not only did it feel like a fingernail, but it hurt. But then how could that be? Dreams don't hurt. Not unless …

'Stinky, I'm talking to you!'

Don't open your eyes, Hugo. Do … not … open … your … eyes.

I slowly opened my eyes and instantly regretted it.

'This can't be happening,' I moaned. I couldn't see properly, not at first, but I still knew who was knelt down beside me … face to face … eye to eye.

'It can be happening,' grinned Fatale De'Ath. 'And that's because it is. I told you I'd see you soon … and here we are. Back together. Best friends forever.'

I chose to ignore her whilst I gathered my thoughts. Where was I? Inside, not out. Sat down, but hunched over. In a chair. Wooden. Old and carved. An antique perhaps. I lifted my head, struggling not to let it drop. The room I was in was dimly lit, but it was big. Really big with a high ceiling. I drew a breath. In through my nose and out through my mouth. That smell. I had been here before. I was sure of it. Quite recently as well.

My brain clicked into gear and the memories came flooding back.

I was in Wildheart Hall. In the Great Room. The last time I had been here was with Poppy. Something had gone wrong, though. What? My eyes shifted and I saw the tatty remains of the suitcase. Of course. There had been a tracker sewn into the lining.

The same tracker that was now hidden down the front of my trousers.

Every second brought a fresh memory. The fire in the barn … my fake funeral … the Bulging Bellyful. That was where Poppy had arranged to meet me. How long ago, however, was anybody's guess. It could've been minutes. Hours. Days. It was impossible to tell and I just couldn't remember. Poppy had been acting strange, though … and then … then … then she had left.

And Mr Skinner and Mr Bones had arrived.

After that I had nothing. No memories. No recollections.

I was just left with a horrible feeling in the pit of my stomach. Horrible *and* all too familiar. A feeling that Poppy had done something I would never have imagined. She had handed me over to Skinner and Bones. I had trusted her and she had betrayed me.

But what did any of that have to do with Fatale De'Ath?

'Are you okay, Stinky?' she asked, placing a hand on my forehead. 'You've gone very pale all of a sudden. You're not going to be sick are you because I've got nothing to clean it up with.'

I shook my head and then attempted to lift my hands so I could rub my eyes. Try as I might, however, I couldn't get them to move. The panic swept over me before I realised they were secured behind my back.

'Would you like me to untie you?' asked Fatale.

'Obviously,' I snapped back at her. 'I mean yes … please. If you could. Sorry. I'm just tired … and confused … *really* confused.'

'Don't be,' insisted Fatale. 'All will be revealed in due course.' She shuffled around to the back of my chair and began to pull at whatever had been used to secure my wrists together. 'You won't try and run off, will you?' she said sternly. 'Because that would be stupid. And you can be quite stupid at times.'

'No, I won't *try* and run off,' I muttered. 'I'll just run off. And that'll be the last you ever see of me.'

'Good joke.' Fatale stood up and patted me on the shoulder. 'There you go,' she said cheerfully. 'All free. Would you like me to help you to your feet?'

217

I shook my head and tried to stand by myself, but only made it halfway up before my legs gave way. 'I think I'll just sit,' I said stubbornly.

At least I had a clear view of my surroundings now. It shocked me to see that, aside from me and Fatale, there were two other people in the Great Room. One was Mr Skinner. With his back against the wall and his eyes staring up at the ceiling, he looked as if he could fall asleep at any moment. No, that was just what he wanted us to think. That he was bored, disinterested by the whole thing. Look a little closer, however, and he was actually tapping his feet whilst he picked at his fingernails. If anything, he seemed on edge. Almost as if he'd rather not be there.

Fatale walked back into my line of sight and I grabbed her by the wrist. 'Why am I here?' I asked.

'It's got nothing to do with her.'

The reply belonged to Layla Krool. She was the second person in the Great Room. Stood in the shadows, she was dressed identically to Fatale (all in black) from the heels of her boots to the tips of her short, spiky hair. The first (and only) time we had met she had fooled me into believing that she was just like me. A spy. And that she worked for SICK.

She didn't, of course. And she wasn't a spy either. I knew that now.

Things were starting to take shape. There was someone missing from this little gathering ... and it wasn't Mr Bones. At a guess, he was probably off digging in the mud. Or scratching his fleas. Or watering a lamppost.

No, the someone who was missing was far more

important than anybody else in attendance. He was both smart and scary. Powerful and poisonous. I had never met him – not properly at least – but I had a horrible feeling that was about to change.

'How much longer do we have to wait?' asked Skinner, shuffling nervously on the spot.

'Not long now,' insisted Krool.

'I can't stand around all day,' Skinner griped. 'I have places to be and people to see. I don't like—'

'Silence,' spat Krool, raising her hand. 'I think … yes, this is it. This is the moment we've all been waiting for. Let the show begin.'

Fatale sat down beside me and groaned.

'What's going on?' I asked.

'Wait and see,' said Fatale, rolling her eyes theatrically. 'Prepare to be entertained … *not*!'

35.'NEVER SAY NEVER.'

I was about to ask Fatale De'Ath what she meant when I heard a strange crackling sound.

It was coming from two large speakers at the other end of the Great Room. They hadn't been there before, I was sure of it. So, why were they here now?

The answer to that curious little question came a moment later when the crackling stopped, only to be replaced by the pounding beat of furious drums. They were soon accompanied by a heavy bass, funky guitars, swirling keyboards and a sweet female voice. I listened carefully as the same lyrics were repeated over and over again.

'He's a bad man, badder than bad,
He's a bad, bad man, don't wanna' make him mad.'

Layla Krool began to clap her hands in time with the music. She scowled at Mr Skinner, who pulled a face before reluctantly joining in.

'This is so embarrassing,' muttered Fatale under her breath.

'What is?' I asked.

'*That.*' Fatale gestured towards the door as, right on cue, a figure emerged through the opening.

It was a man. Tall and thin with razor sharp features, pouty lips and black, silky hair that ran all the way down his back, I watched in amazement as he danced into the Great Room with his eyes closed and his arms swirling above his head. He was dressed in a flowery shirt and white leather trousers. Despite the chill in the air, his feet were bare and his toenails were painted red.

I poked Fatale to get her attention. 'Is this the entertainment you were talking about?'

'Regrettably so,' she replied. 'He always does this. He says he likes to make an entrance. I'm the only one who dares to tell him how ridiculous he looks, though.'

I screwed up my face, more confused than ever. 'Who is he?'

'That's my father,' revealed Fatale.

'Your father?' I repeated. 'But your father is Deadly De'Ath?'

'I knew you'd get there in the end,' muttered Fatale. 'That man is my father and my father is Deadly De'Ath. Would you like me to write it down for you in case you forget?'

No, I didn't need it in writing … but that didn't mean I was entirely convinced either. Deadly De'Ath was both a criminal mastermind and the most feared man in Crooked Elbow. People were absolutely terrified of him. The only thing terrifying about the man stood before me, however, was his dancing.

'Is this a joke?' I asked.

'No joke,' said Fatale, shaking her pigtails. 'I'll prove it if you don't believe me.'

With that, she marched over to the speakers and pulled both sockets out of the wall. As expected, the music ground to a sudden halt, much to the dancing man's disgust.

'Not cool, Fatale,' he grumbled. When he opened his eyes they were as dark as the night sky. 'Not cool at all. I was enjoying that.'

'You might have been, but I wasn't,' Fatale scowled. 'It was getting boring. Besides, I've got a question. Who are you?'

'Who am I?' The dancing man put his hands on his hips and stuck out his chin. 'You heard the song,' he replied. 'I'm bad. Bad to the bone and twice as evil.'

'Yes, I know that,' groaned Fatale. 'But who *are* you?'

'I'm your worst nightmare,' laughed the dancing man. 'Nasty not nice. Sour not sweet. Wicked not—'

'You're repeating yourself now,' Fatale sighed. 'Just tell me who you are.'

'Stop this!' A raging Layla Krool began to stride across the Great Room. 'How dare you speak to your father like that!'

'My father!' Fatale turned and wagged a finger in my face. 'Told you, Stinky.'

I stared at her in disbelief. So it was true. The dancing man in the middle of the Great Room really was Deadly De'Ath.

And now Deadly De'Ath was swaggering towards me.

222

'Stinky?' he remarked. 'Stinky makes Pinky and Pinky makes Pink Weasel. You're Hugo Dare. The spy they've all been searching for.'

The only way to answer that was with a shrug.

'Don't be so modest,' smirked De'Ath. 'If it wasn't for you, none of us would even be here. Which reminds me ...' De'Ath spun around on the spot. 'You won,' he cried, pointing with both hands at Mr Skinner. 'You beat all the others. You and your hairy friend ... you found Hugo Dare and brought him to me. You must be the happiest man ... with a dog who's not really a dog ... in the whole of Crooked Elbow.'

Mr Skinner loosened his collar and tried to breathe. 'I am, Your Deadliness,' he said gruffly. 'Whatever you say.'

'Whatever I say?' De'Ath ran a long fingernail over his unnaturally smooth skin. 'I like the sound of that,' he nodded. 'And you should like the sound of this. The moment has come for you to accept your prize. You know what to do, my fumbling friend ...'

A jittery Mr Skinner tried to swallow before he dropped down onto one knee. Stepping forward, Deadly De'Ath clenched his fist as he held out his hand. There was a large, square-shaped ring resting on his middle finger, which Skinner gently kissed.

'Thank you, Your Deadliness,' he said, his metal leg knocking against the floor as he clambered to his feet. 'It's a wonderful prize. I'm grateful beyond words. Now, if there's nothing else then I think I'll be on my—'

'What was that?' I blurted out.

'Shush,' said a furious Krool, glaring at me from afar.

'No, you shush,' I shot back at her. 'All weekend I've been running around in circles ... and squares ... and the occasional triangle ... and for what? So grumpy old Mr Skinner could plant a sloppy kiss on that garish ring? What kind of prize is that?'

'It's a mark of respect,' explained Fatale. 'Mr Skinner is under my father's protection now. No harm can ever come to him. He's part of the inner circle. He's a disciple of De'Ath.'

Mr Skinner seemed happy enough with that and limped hastily out of the Great Room.

'Good for Skinner,' I moaned. 'But what's any of this got to do with me? And where's Poppy?'

'Poppy's dead,' replied De'Ath. There was a strained silence before he started to laugh. 'Not really,' he admitted. 'I was just being funny. I am funny, aren't I? I've never even met this Poppy, but Mr Skinner told me this was her house. That was why I moved in. Not forever, of course. Just a temporary dwelling. So, who is she? Your auntie? Your favourite teacher? Your pet goldfish? Or just a grotesque combination of all three?'

'She's a friend,' I declared.

'Like me,' chipped-in Fatale.

'Not a bit like you,' I said, correcting her. 'Poppy may have her faults, but I doubt she'd ever hold me hostage whilst a strange man dances in front of me—'

Twirling a finger, Deadly De'Ath pretended to wipe a tear from his eye. 'I thought you liked the dancing,' he said sadly.

'He does,' replied Krool, answering for me.

'He probably doesn't,' argued Fatale.

'No, I *definitely* don't,' I insisted. 'It's weird.' I watched as Deadly De'Ath sashayed towards me with his hand outstretched. 'And things are only about to get a whole lot weirder ...'

'It's your turn,' announced De'Ath. I leant back in my chair as he drew uncomfortably close. 'That's the reason you're here, after all,' he said softly. 'It's also why I've had some of the most fearsome felons and freaks in Crooked Elbow hunt you down. I ... no, *we* want you to be like us. Kiss my hand and you can be part of my inner circle. You, too, can be a disciple of De'Ath.'

I screwed up my face. 'And why would I possibly want to do that?'

'Because of Fatale,' remarked De'Ath, gesturing flamboyantly towards his daughter. 'Ever since I escaped from the Crooked Clink, she hasn't stopped talking about you. She said you were her favourite person in Elbow's End. So I said, what about me? And she said, no, it was most certainly you. So I said, really? And she said, yes, really. So I said, what about my feelings? And she said I don't care about your—'

'I'm not going to be like you,' I said, butting-in.

Deadly De'Ath stepped back in amazement. 'Wow!'

'I told you he'd say that,' moaned Fatale. 'He's too nice. He's a spy for the good guys.'

'Big deal,' shrugged De'Ath. 'Spies are just nosey. Well, Stinky can be nosey for us. He can be my little spy.'

'Never,' I shouted. The word had escaped from my

mouth without me realising. Now I did realise, however, I decided to say it three more times. 'Never … never … never!'

'Never say never,' said De'Ath.

'I just did,' I insisted. 'And so did you. Twice.'

'You might change your mind,' said Fatale. 'I do. All the time. No one would care—'

'I'd care,' I cried. 'It'd go against everything I stand for. I can't think of anything worse than joining your father's inner circle.'

'I can.' Layla Krool rubbed her hands together as she wandered towards me. 'Let me show you how we deal with people who refuse to bow down to the great Deadly De'Ath.'

'Wait!' insisted Fatale, leaping in front of me. 'Let's give him one last chance.'

'I don't need it,' I said stubbornly.

'Yes, you do,' argued Fatale. 'Maybe you'd like to go away and think about things.'

'Or maybe I wouldn't,' I snapped back at her.

Fatale threw her hands up in despair. 'Oh, Stinky, will you please shut up?' she cried. 'I'm trying to help you.'

'I don't need any help,' I said stubbornly.

'Well, I think you do,' argued Fatale.

'And I *know* you do.'

I looked beyond his daughter and saw Deadly De'Ath as he emerged from the shadows. The sight of him was enough to make me shiver. He had changed. Not in appearance, but in manner. The twirling and swirling, the pouting and pointing, all of it had been replaced by something much darker and far more menacing.

'If you don't want to join us then I suppose I have no further use for you,' he said coldly.

'Really?' I said, jumping up. 'I can see myself out. You don't have to show me to the—'

Quick as a flash, Krool rushed forward and pushed me back down onto my chair.

'Nice try, Stinky,' sighed Fatale, 'but that's not what my father means.'

'Your time here is drawing to an end,' began De'Ath. 'You're no longer required. And what do we do with things we no longer require? We dispose of them … forever.'

I tried to swallow, but my throat had dried up. Which got me thinking …

'Can I have some water please?' I asked innocently.

Layla Krool grabbed a vase from one of the many tables, threw the dead flowers over her shoulder and then handed it to me. 'Have this,' she grinned. 'There's some water in the bottom. It might be a little stale, but it's all you deserve.'

'It'll do.' Pressing the vase to my lips, I pretended to drink before placing it down by my feet.

'Savour the taste because that's the last water that will ever pass your lips,' declared De'Ath, striding towards me with his arms outstretched. This time, however, he had no intention of letting me kiss his hand. 'Any last requests?'

'Just the one,' I said hastily. 'You might think this a little unusual, but …' Slowly, so not to cause alarm, I reached into my pocket and removed the tube of toothpaste my father had given me. You do remember the toothpaste, don't you?

The exploding toothpaste.

'You want to brush your teeth?' sniggered Krool.

'Why not?' I lifted the lid and squeezed the bottom of the tube before anyone could disagree. If this was going to work then I had to time it to perfection. What's that? No, of course I'm not really going to brush my teeth. That would just be ridiculous.

'What are you waiting for?' spat Krool.

'The right moment,' I replied.

Dangling the toothpaste above the vase, I took aim ... and then let go of the entire tube. My heart leapt as it landed with a wet *plop*. There. I had done it. Now all I had to do was sit back and wait for the explosion.

I was still waiting when Deadly De'Ath broke the silence.

'Well, that was a bit silly, wasn't it?' he said, confused. 'If I didn't know any better I'd say you did that on purpose.'

I was about to plead my innocence when the vase began to violently shake. I began to shuffle backwards before it did something that nobody would ever have predicted.

Nobody except me.

I was still shuffling when the vase stopped shaking ... and exploded!

Boom time!

36.'PINK WEASEL IS NOT FOR TURNING.'

When my father had shown me the exploding toothpaste in our garden, he had only used a tiny blob.

I, however, used the entire tube.

And the result was absolute devastation.

The moment it exploded I was thrown backwards off my chair into the wall behind me. I landed with a bump, but I wasn't alone. When I had finally mustered the strength to look again, Fatale, Layla Krool and, perhaps most importantly, Deadly De'Ath had all been swept off their feet and left in a heap by the powerful blast. Smoke filtered down to where I lay and I lost sight of each of them.

If ever there was a time to get out of there it was now.

Getting out of anywhere, however, largely requires you to know where you're going … and I didn't. The smoke was so thick by now that I could barely see beyond my own nose. I lifted my hand and waved it in front of my face, but it made no difference. Then it hit me. No, not my own hand. An idea.

'We're under attack!' I yelled. Wait ... 'No, *you're* under attack!' I said, correcting myself. 'They're not interested in me.'

Ducking below the smoke, I laid flat on my stomach and saw movement across the Great Room. It was Layla Krool. She was crawling towards something that I couldn't quite make out. Some kind of flowery heap. The smoke shifted a little and I saw that it was Deadly De'Ath. Pushing himself up, the two of them began to whisper. Planning their escape, no doubt.

One person, however, was still yet to stir.

Without thinking, I fought my way through the debris in search of Fatale. Despite the smoke, it didn't take me long to find her. Flat on her back with her eyes closed and her arms by her side, she looked peaceful laid out on the rug. Almost *too* peaceful.

I had a sudden urge to shake her, but decided instead to simply run a hand over her forehead. To my relief she opened her eyes and smiled.

'I don't know how you did that, Stinky,' she said quietly, 'but it was awesome!'

I was about to reply when the Great Room was rocked by another explosion. This time, however, it had nothing to do with me. Or my father's exploding toothpaste.

No, this was real.

'We're under attack!' I shouted.

'You've already said that!' Krool yelled back at me.

'Yes, but this time I'm telling the truth!' I threw myself on top of Fatale as the windows caved in behind us. Whoever it was, they were trying desperately to get inside Wildheart Hall. Trying *and* succeeding by the look of things.

'We can't let them find you here, Your Deadliness,' insisted Krool. With a hand on Deadly De'Ath's elbow, she began to guide him towards the open doorway. 'You're still on the run, remember? You're a wanted man.'

'How could I forget?' sighed De'Ath. Moving cautiously through the smoke, he had almost made it outside when he turned back into the Great Room. 'Come quickly, Fatale. It is time for us to depart.'

A determined Fatale pushed me away so she could sit up. 'I'm not going anywhere,' she replied. 'Not without Stinky. We have to take him with us.'

There was another loud explosion and the ceiling began to shudder.

'Leave him to rot,' ordered De'Ath, waving her pleas away. 'He's not one of us and he never will be. Pink Weasel is not for turning.'

With that, Deadly De'Ath pushed past Krool before hurrying out of the Great Room.

For all her bluster, I could tell that Fatale was about to follow her father. Scrambling to her feet, she hesitated just long enough for me to grab her by the arm.

'Stinky!' she cried. 'Let go of me!'

'I would if I could but I can't,' I insisted. 'We need you. You can help us get to Deadly De'Ath. You are his daughter, after all.'

'I'm also your friend,' remarked Fatale.

I ducked down as another explosion rocked the house.

Shaken by the blast, I released Fatale's arm at the same time and expected her to run. Curiously, she didn't.

'A friend would never have treated me like you did,' I moaned. 'I've been hunted and hounded all weekend by the Undesirable Eight. I even had to fake my own death … and it was all because of you!'

'Me?' Fatale opened her mouth to argue, but then thought better of it. 'Maybe you're right. Maybe it was my fault. And I'm sorry. But I only did it because I wanted you to join us. Part of me even thought you might, Pinky … but I was wrong.'

That took me by surprise. No, not the apology. 'Did you just call me Pinky?' I asked.

'Why wouldn't I?' grinned Fatale. 'That is your name, after all.' She stopped smiling and glanced over at the door. 'I need to go … please.'

'Okay,' I nodded. 'I'll let you. But not before you've made me a promise.'

'Anything.' Fatale covered her face as another window exploded and shards of glass flew across the room. 'Just make it quick, eh?'

'Promise that you'll never try anything like this again,' I said firmly. 'I mean it, Fatale. No more hunting me down. No more winners and losers. And definitely no more kissing that ring. Do you understand?'

'Fine,' shrugged Fatale. 'I promise. And now I've really got to—' She was about to race towards the door when I grabbed her again.

'Not that way.' I kept hold of her arm as I scrambled to

my feet and hurried towards the other end of the Great Room. I stopped at the suit of armour and touched the tip of the sword. Right on cue, the door began to open and the secret tunnel revealed itself. 'This leads all the way into the grounds of Wildheart Hall,' I explained. 'You'll be safe from there.'

Fatale slipped through the entrance without another word … and then came back a moment later. 'I forgot to say thank you,' she said. 'So … um … thank you. Until we meet again …'

I screwed up my face as she finally left for good. 'Yeah, can't wait,' I muttered to myself. I touched the tip of the sword again and the door closed. The secret tunnel had disappeared. And so, too, had Fatale De'Ath.

I had barely turned away from the wall when a furious burst of activity in the Great Room forced me to dive for cover. Laid flat out on the rug, I watched in amazement as hordes of shadowy figures swarmed in through the smashed windows. With the smoke still yet to fully disperse, all I could see were their face masks, padded vests and weapons. Guns mostly.

I stayed down until I heard a voice I recognised.

'Get up, young Dare! You're making the place look untidy.'

That wasn't strictly true. The place was untidy already. That didn't stop me, however, from sitting up and smiling at the man who was stood over me.

'It's good to see you,' boomed the Big Cheese. 'Well, not good. Just average. Perfectly satisfactory. Now, where are the others?'

'What others?' I shrugged.

'The odious others,' explained the Big Cheese. 'The bad guys. The naughty people. Don't tell me you've been here on your own all along.'

'I wasn't … but I am now,' I revealed. 'Believe it or not, but Deadly De'Ath was here before.'

'Deadly De'Ath?' The Big Cheese groaned like the weary walrus he undoubtedly was. 'We've missed him, haven't we?'

'Only just,' I replied. 'He's not been gone long. You could always try and—'

The Big Cheese refused to let me finish my sentence as he rushed out of the Great Room in search of SICK's number one enemy. He was followed by every one of the masked figures. It was only when they had all gone that I noticed there was still one person remaining.

And that person was Poppy.

'Is it safe to come in?' she asked warily.

'It is now,' I said, climbing to my feet. 'How did you know where to find me?'

Poppy pointed at the lump in my trousers. 'The tracker,' she revealed. 'I rearranged the settings before I gave it to you. It allowed us to follow your every move. We saw they had brought you here … to my house of all places … and then we planned our attack. We got here just in time by the look of things.' Poppy hesitated. 'Don't think bad of me, Hugo,' she said. 'I know it was the wrong thing to do … but I did it for all the right reasons.'

I screwed up my face. I had mixed emotions and I didn't like it. Yes, I was still mad with Poppy, but at least I was safe now.

'I knew the whole fake funeral thing wouldn't work,' began Poppy. 'I mean, what were you supposed to do? Hide away in the SICK Bucket for the rest of your life?'

'I tried that and didn't even last one day,' I sighed.

'Exactly,' nodded Poppy. 'That's why I wanted to try something different. Something like telling Mr Skinner and Mr Bones where to find you. I used you as bait, Hugo. I'm not proud of myself, but I thought it was the only way we could catch them in the act. Then it would all be over.' Poppy paused. 'The thing is, it's not, is it? We haven't caught anybody and we won't now either. I'm sorry, Hugo, but nothing has changed. As soon as you leave here they'll come again and—'

'They won't,' I said firmly.

'You don't know that.' Poppy eyed me with suspicion. 'Do you?'

I thought about Fatale and what she had promised. Strange as it seems, I believed her.

'Yes, I do,' I insisted. 'The hunt for Hugo Dare is well and truly over. I'm certain of it. Now, let's get out of here whilst we still can,' I said, heading towards the exit. 'I don't know about you, Pops, but I'm absolutely starving … and, no offence, but fish paste chocolate biscuits just don't quite hit the spot!'

37. 'I'LL SEE YOU WHEN IT'S OVER.'

Fifteen hours later I met Poppy outside The Impossible Pizza takeaway.

She was pacing up and down with her eyes glued to the pavement (not really) and a deep frown carved into her forehead (not really again). Both worried me instantly. Where was her usual smile? Her high spirits? Her endless enthusiasm?

She saw me and stopped pacing. 'You've come.'

'I said I would,' I replied.

'Yes, you did,' nodded Poppy, 'but I still wasn't expecting you to show. Nobody would ever know if you hadn't bothered.'

'I'd know.' I took in my surroundings as we talked. It was Monday morning, the crack of dawn. The streets were deserted and there was nobody in sight. 'Where's the Big Cheese?' I asked.

'Still in bed I'd imagine,' admitted Poppy. 'He doesn't know that you're here ... and I don't think he'd be happy if he did! You should really be resting after everything that's happened.' Poppy placed a hand on my shoulder. 'You don't have to do this.'

'I do,' I said stubbornly.

'No, you don't,' Poppy insisted. 'It's not safe, Hugo. I'd almost say it's potentially life-threatening.'

I shushed her mid-sentence. I felt bad enough already and she was only making things worse. 'Is anybody else coming?' I asked instead.

Poppy pulled a face. 'I called them, but they all refused,' she revealed. 'They said it was too dangerous. You can hardly blame them.'

'I don't,' I shrugged. And that much was true. I mean, how could I? What I was about to do went well beyond the call of duty. It was horrendously hazardous. Perilously precarious. So ridiculously risky that only a complete and utter bird brain would even consider it. Yes, I do realise what that makes me. I'm not stupid.

Well, not much anyway.

Poppy drew a breath. 'I suppose … I could always—'

'No, you can't,' I said, shaking my head. 'This isn't your battle, Pops. Don't fret; it won't take me long. I'll get in, do the job and get out. It's that simple.'

'If only,' muttered Poppy.

I tried to snatch a breath. 'I'll see you when it's over. Keep your fingers crossed.'

'I'll keep my fingers crossed if you keep your eyes peeled,' replied Poppy. 'One wrong move could be fatal.' She took a moment, the worry evident on her face. 'Go get 'em, Agent Minus Thirty-Five,' she said at last.

I quickly turned away and set off across the road before nerves got the better of me. I had almost reached the opposite side when the door to the Bulging Bellyful swung open.

'Get shiftin'!' yelled Grot, beckoning me inside. 'This place won't clean itself.'

I knew that already, but thanks for reminding me.

'It's an absolute disaster zone,' Grot continued. 'And it stinks. Worse than ever. If anythin', it reminds me of Grunt's breath when he brushes his teeth in the toilet.' Grot hesitated. 'Ya are still comin' to help, aren't ya?' she asked. 'A promise is a promise, after all.'

'I'm here, aren't I?' I said grumpily. At the same time I pulled on a pair of rubber gloves ... before pulling on another pair just to be extra careful.

'Everythin' we need is inside,' revealed Grot. 'We've got mops and buckets. Dustpans and brushes. Cloths and wipes. A flame thrower—'

I screwed up my face. 'A flame thrower?'

'Some of those stains are pretty tricky to get off,' explained Grot. 'Right, I think that's about it ...'

'Not quite.' I was stood on the doorstep, but I wasn't quite ready to go in yet. 'There's something I need to tell you,' I began. 'If I don't make it out of here alive—'

'Don't talk like that,' butted in Grot.

'Yes, I know,' I sighed. 'It upsets me too.'

'No, it's not that,' cried Grot. 'It's ma bladder. I'm burstin' for a piddle. If I'm not careful I'll start leakin' all over the pavement ... and that's a sight nobody wants to see!'

With that, Grot shoved me to one side as she shuffled

back inside the Bulging Bellyful. I took a moment to wave wearily at Poppy and then followed her through the door.

This was it. There was no turning back now. I'll see you on the other side.

If I make it that far, of course …

THE END

HUGO DARE WILL RETURN

IN…

ESCAPE FROM
ODD ISLAND

OTHER BOOKS IN THE SERIES

THE GREATEST SPY WHO NEVER WAS
(HUGO DARE BOOK 1)

Meet Hugo Dare. Schoolboy turned super spy. Both stupidly dangerous and dangerously stupid.

A robbery at the Bottle Bank. Diamond smuggling at the Pearly Gates Cemetery. The theft of priceless artefact, Coocamba's Idol. Hugo is there on each and every occasion. but then so, too, is someone else.

Wrinkles, the town of Crooked Elbow's oldest criminal mastermind.

In a battle of good versus evil, young versus old, ugly versus even uglier, there can only be one winner … and it better be Hugo otherwise we're all in trouble!

To buy in the US - The Greatest Spy Who Never Was (Hugo Dare Book 1) - Kindle edition by Codd, David. Children Kindle eBooks @ Amazon.com.

To buy in the UK - The Greatest Spy Who Never Was (Hugo Dare Book 1) eBook: Codd, David: Amazon.co.uk: Kindle Store

THE WEASEL HAS LANDED
(HUGO DARE BOOK 2)

Schoolboy turned super spy Hugo Dare is back ... and this time he's going where others fear to tread!

No, not barefoot through a puddle of cat sick. This is much, much worse than that.

Maya, the Mayor of Crooked Elbow's daughter, is being held captive in one of the most dangerous places known to mankind.

Elbow's End.

Populated by rogues and wrong 'uns of the lowest order, only one person can find Maya and get her out of there in one piece. Unfortunately, that person is busy flossing their nostrils so it's left to someone else.

And that someone else is Hugo!

To buy in the US – The Weasel Has Landed (Hugo Dare Book 2) - Kindle edition by Codd, David. Children Kindle eBooks @ Amazon.com.

To buy in the UK – The Weasel Has Landed (Hugo Dare Book 2) eBook: Codd, David: Amazon.co.uk: Kindle Store

THE DAY OF THE RASCAL (HUGO DARE BOOK 3)

Teenage super spy Hugo Dare returns. That's the good news. The bad news is he's faced with his perilous mission yet. We'll come to that in a moment …

The Day of the Rascal. A day when the whole of Crooked Elbow falls foul to the devilish antics of one devious little delinquent. The year, however, the Rascal has turned the screw. No more childish pranks and elaborate stunts for him. No, this year he plans to take out the Chief of SICK … and I don't mean for dinner! He wants to finish him off. Eliminate, eradicate and exterminate. RIP the Big Cheese.

Hugo is soon on the case. His instructions are simple. Stop the Rascal before it's too late. Easy-peasy. With any luck he might even be home in time for breakfast.

If only that was true …

To buy in the US - The Day Of The Rascal (Hugo Dare Book 3) - Kindle edition by Codd, David. Children Kindle eBooks @ Amazon.com.

To buy in the UK - The Day Of The Rascal (Hugo Dare Book 3) eBook: Codd, David: Amazon.co.uk: Kindle Store

ACKNOWLEDGEMENTS

Thanks to the wonderful Sian Phillips for her eagle-eyed editing skills and glowing praise.

Thanks to the wonderful Stuart Bache and all the team at Books Covered for the front cover.

Thanks to everyone at the wonderful Polgarus Studio for their first-rate formatting.

Note to self – look for another word other than wonderful. Do not forget. Because that would be really embarrassing. I'm embarrassed enough already just thinking about it.

AUTHOR FACTFILE

NAME: David Codd. But you can call me David Codd. Because that's my name. Obviously.

DATE OF BIRTH: Sometime in the past. It's all a little hazy. I'm not entirely convinced I was even there if I'm being honest.

BIRTHPLACE: In a hospital. In Lincoln. In Lincolnshire. In England.

ADDRESS: No, thank you. I don't like the feel of the wind against my bare legs.

HEIGHT: Taller than a squirrel but much shorter than a lamppost. Just somewhere in between.

WEIGHT: What for?

OCCUPATION: Writing this. It doesn't just happen by accident. Or does it?

LIKES: Norwich City football club, running, desert boots, parsnips.

DISLIKES: Norwich City football club, running, rain, Brussels sprouts.

REASON FOR WRITING: My fingers needed some exercise. They were getting lazy, just hanging there, doing nothing.

ANYTHING ELSE: Thank you for reading this book. If you've got this far then you deserve a medal. Just don't ask me for one. Because I haven't got any. But I am very grateful. And do feel free to leave a review on Amazon if leaving reviews on Amazon is your kind of thing. It's not easy for a new author so please be kind.

Until the next time …

Printed in Great Britain
by Amazon